BENOTRIPIA
THE RESCUE

MCKENZIE WAGNER

BENOTRIPIA
THE RESCUE

MCKENZIE WAGNER

Sweetwater Books
An Imprint of Cedar Fort, Inc.
Springville, Utah

ISBN 13: 978-1-4621-1014-8

Published by Sweetwater Books, an imprint of Cedar Fort, Inc.
2373 W. 700 S., Springville, UT 84663
Distributed by Cedar Fort, Inc., www.cedarfort.com

LIBRARY OF CONGRESS CATALOGING-IN-PUBLICATION DATA

Wagner, Mckenzie, 2000- author.
  The rescue / Mckenzie Wagner.
     pages cm
  Roseabelle and two friends, Astro and Jessicana, embark on a perilous journey to Darvonia to save her mother and, if possible, their homeland, Benotripia.
  ISBN 978-1-4621-1014-8 (alk. paper)
  1. Children's writings, American. [1. Fantasy. 2. Children's writings.] I. Title.

  PZ7.W1245Re 2012
  [Fic]--dc23

                              2012021704

Cover design by Brian Halley
Cover design © 2012 Lyle Mortimer
Edited and typeset by Emily S. Chambers

Printed in the United States of America

10 9 8 7 6 5 4 3 2 1

Printed on acid-free paper

Contents

Prologue

I T WAS A CHILLY NIGHT—CHILLY FOR THE TROPI-
cal island of Benotripia. There were no clouds, how-
ever, and no cold winds swept the air.

Under the starry night sky, a woman made her way
cautiously across a white, starlit beach. The waves lapped
gently against smooth, gray rocks, and the moonlight
glinted in the woman's silky honey-colored hair.

As soon as she reached the water's edge, she stopped.
There was complete silence—save for the waves continu-
ing their tireless routine of rolling in across the beach. A
few tiny waves of water reached the woman's ankles, but
she took no notice.

The woman sighed. It was a beautiful night. She
wished her husband could be here to see it. But then,
he could be looking at the stars right now also. She only
wished she knew where he was.

Heavy footsteps sounded through the darkness, shattering her thoughts, and she looked around apprehensively. A tall red-headed man appeared almost instantly by her side, and she sighed with relief.

"I'm glad you could come," she whispered. "Especially after the tragedy that happened this morning." Even in the darkness, the woman could see the look of utter confusion on his face. She was surprised he didn't know.

"What are you speaking of?" the man whispered back with concern.

"Magford. He's gone."

"What?"

"Gone. Without a trace."

"Do you have any ideas how it . . . ?" He trailed off as a noiseless crystal tear trickled down the woman's cheek. "Leader Danette, we will find him. I promise. You will not be the only leader of Benotripia for long," the man vowed.

The woman nodded with a weak smile and hastily wiped the tear off her cheek.

"How is Roseabelle?" the man whispered, referring to her two-year-old daughter.

"She doesn't know yet—she's too young to understand," the woman answered. "Losing a parent is a terrible fate."

The man nodded again. "It is probably better that she doesn't know. I will aid your daughter in any way I can. She will need help as she grows."

"Thank you. For everything."

Without another word, the man slipped away into the shadows of the slightly swaying palm trees.

CHAPTER 1

Roseabelle

"ROSEABELLE, IT'S TIME FOR TRAINING," Danette called up the stairs. "If you don't hurry, you'll be late."

Roseabelle quickly sat up in bed.

When Benotripians reached eight years old, they started school at one of Benotripia's many power training academies. Every student had his or her own personal trainer, and since Roseabelle had been at the Central Power Training Academy for two years, she had developed a personal bond with Shelby, her trainer.

She hastily dressed into her crimson sports dress and slid her feet into black slip-on shoes. After brushing her long, auburn hair and pulling it back with a red ribbon, she zipped downstairs and grabbed her water bottle.

"Train hard," Danette encouraged.

"I will," Roseabelle answered.

As Danette exited the room, Roseabelle strode to the shadow falling behind the wooden steps. When she was nine years old, she had learned to shadow tumble. Shadow tumbling was one of the uncommon powers that Roseabelle had since she had Meta-Mord. Meta-Mord was extremely rare, and it bestowed Roseabelle with many unique powers.

The required actions of shadow tumbling were to fully immerse yourself in a shadow and picture a place where you wanted to go. You could travel through the shadow and arrive at the place you had pictured—or at least in a shadow nearby.

Roseabelle stepped into the shadow. She pictured Central Power Training Academy and thumped her foot. She felt herself being whisked away, and before she knew it, she had landed smoothly on the soft soil.

She opened her eyes and saw herself standing next to the magnificent structure of Central Power Training Academy. She saw kids piling in through the front doors. Memories flooded back to Roseabelle. Here at the academy she and her friends had learned how to use and fight with weapons and had studied more about their powers.

Among the crowd of students, Roseabelle spotted Jessicana and Astro, her best friends.

Jessicana had long, blonde hair and aqua-blue eyes

and was wearing a bright red and orange shirt, lemon-yellow tights, and a short green and blue skirt. Her shoes matched her eyes.

In contrast, Astro had spiky jet-black hair and alert green eyes. He was wearing a black T-shirt with waves of blue on it and a pair of jeans. Matching blue and black flip-flops completed his outfit.

Jessicana and Astro each had one power. Jessicana could shape-shift into a parrot, and Astro could shoot lightning bolts from his fingertips.

"Hey, Roseabelle! Over here!" Astro called. Roseabelle streaked past the throng of people.

"How's it going?" Roseabelle asked earnestly.

"Fine, I guess," Jessicana said.

"Come on. We had better get checked in," Astro said.

They entered the academy. It really was a stunning sight. The entire building was built out of polished white marble. With its 244 rooms and its majestic balconies, the Central Power Training Academy was one of the grandest Academies in Benotripia.

Roseabelle, Astro, and Jessicana signed in on the register and turned to find Shelby, Polly (Astro's trainer), and Asteran (Jessicana's trainer) waiting for them.

"Better get going," the three friends muttered simultaneously. Shelby led Roseabelle to a large room on the fourth floor, labeled "Creature Care." Shelby opened the door and beckoned for Roseabelle to come inside.

The room was filled with all sorts of animals—ordinary and magical. Cages lined the walls, containing toucans, red-eyed tree frogs, and boa constrictors. Tanks full of water housed various kinds of colorful fish and crabs. A small fence surrounded a creature with meaty legs, a tall oval body, sharp five-fingered claws, and a round pudgy face with a snout and three beady eyes.

Shelby turned to Roseabelle. "You might know that Meta-Mords have the ability to sense animals' emotions and feelings. Today we will work on this," Shelby explained.

"First, we will start with the mottel on the window over there." She nodded to a window with a flat wooden board attached. On it rested a bird with a soft middle and round, bumpy toes. It had a sharp beak, two round eyes, brightly colored feathers, and large rounded wings.

Roseabelle knew a little about mottels. They were native birds that spoke messages. A person would tell the mottel the message, and then the small bird would fly off to the person who was to receive the message. The mottel would repeat what it had heard and then fly away. Roseabelle knew that Jessicana's mother kept some for pets.

Roseabelle ran over to the window and was shortly joined by Shelby.

"Put your hand on the mottel," Shelby instructed. Roseabelle did. "Now block out every little bit of sound you hear. Pretend you are alone with the mottel. No one there. No one," Shelby said hypnotically.

Roseabelle tried her best and put all her focus on the mottel, which was watching her curiously.

"All right, are you getting anything?" Shelby asked. Roseabelle closed her eyes. Nothing so far. She didn't feel anything different.

Roseabelle started to get a little jumpy and eager. She wanted to get up and move around. She had to! Something was holding her down. She didn't want that. But what was it?

Suddenly Shelby's voice broke through her thoughts. "Are you feeling any peculiar emotions?"

Roseabelle opened her eyes. "Yes," she said. "I'm feeling like I need to move around. I want to but something is holding me down."

Shelby nodded. "That is probably what the mottel is feeling. The something that is holding it down is your hand. You did good, Roseabelle. Which animal do you want to try next?" Shelby questioned.

For the next hour or so, Roseabelle practiced feeling the emotions of other animals. She gradually and naturally excelled at it. When she asked Shelby if she could practice on the ugly animal locked in the fence, Shelby turned white and hissed, "No!"

Roseabelle was surprised. "Uh, okay," she said, slightly taken back.

Instead, she walked to a spotted juddle—a mammal

with leathery skin, almond-shaped eyes, and sticklike legs.

At lunchtime, Shelby dismissed her, and Roseabelle fled down the stairs. She sped into the bright cafeteria and quickly spotted Astro in the back of the lunch line. She grabbed a lunch tray and joined him.

"Have you seen Jessicana?" Roseabelle asked.

"No," Astro said simply.

But it wasn't hard to find Jessicana in her bright clothing. The parrot-girl soon walked into line.

"There you are," Roseabelle said with relief. But Jessicana didn't respond. She was staring at Asteran, her trainer, with concentration. Although puzzled, Roseabelle decided not to disturb Jessicana.

When she reached the food bar, Roseabelle piled butter onto her potatoes, took a fruit cup, and dished herself some yogurt. She then sat down at one of the large lunch tables. All Jessicana took was some fruit and nuts. Astro heaped plates of salad, bowls of soup, and glasses of water on his now heavy tray. He sat next to Roseabelle and began to eat ravenously.

When Astro had finished the last of his soup, Jessicana whispered, "Look at Asteran. Doesn't he seem a little secretive?" Roseabelle looked to where Jessicana was pointing. She was right. The tall trainer was looking around cautiously and clutching his arm. "I'm going to see what he's up to," Jessicana whispered. She started to rise from the table, but Astro took hold of her sleeve.

"What are you thinking? People don't like you prying into their business," Astro urged quietly.

Jessicana shrugged. "I don't think it will hurt. After all, I am his trainee," she reasoned. Astro and Roseabelle shared a look and there was a long pause.

Jessicana tapped her foot on the marble floor, sending an echo across the large cafeteria. "Oh come on, Astro," she said impatiently.

She tried to rise again, but Astro grabbed her sleeve for the second time. "Jessicana, no! What are you thinking?" Astro said, shaking his head.

"Astro," Roseabelle half whispered. "The Darvonians haven't taken any action since m-my father disappeared." Roseabelle took a deep breath at the thought of her father and paused for a minute. "You know what they're like. Their reputation is silence for a few years and then suddenly revealing a well-planned, brilliant scheme. Nothing has happened for eight years. They've had plenty of time to plot something against Benotripia," Roseabelle said. "I just think we should be on our guard about anything suspicious. That's all I'm trying to say."

Astro looked at Roseabelle and sighed. Then he groaned. "All right, all right," Astro said, "but I'm coming with you."

"Me too," added Roseabelle. The three friends rose from the table, placed their dirty lunch trays on the counter, and walked with quick, short steps toward Asteran.

The dark-haired trainer was leaning against the wall, his eyes darting around the cafeteria. Astro, Jessicana, and Roseabelle stood casually next to a slight break in the wall, which hid them from Asteran's view. When Asteran made sure no eyes were looking his way, he slipped out the lunch door.

Roseabelle led her friends out of the cafeteria. She saw Asteran turn into another hallway and then disappear. The trio walked to the end of the hall and turned also. They followed Asteran is this manner, making sure that they weren't seen.

They had traveled through several hallways when Asteran reached a small side door. He opened it and walked silently through. Asteran closed the door behind him and disappeared from the kids' view.

Jessicana transformed into a parrot and rose into the air. "*Awk, awk*, he's up to something," she squawked firmly.

"Why don't you see what he is up to?" Roseabelle asked.

"*Awk*, I will," Jessicana replied. Astro opened the door for her and Jessicana flew in pursuit of Asteran. Astro closed the door.

"Well, we had better get to our trainers. I hope we haven't been gone long," Roseabelle remarked. At that moment, the two heard footsteps.

CHAPTER 2
Followed!

ROSEABELLE GULPED. POLLY APPEARED IN THE hall. "Astro, there you are! And Roseabelle. I'm sorry, dear, but Shelby unexpectedly left. Haven't got a clue of where she went. Your mother will be informed of this. You may go. Now, Astro, back to the weather room," Polly said apologetically.

She beckoned for Astro to follow her. When Polly turned away, Roseabelle mouthed, "Meet me at my house." Astro nodded and walked away with Polly.

Roseabelle opened the door and walked out. She looked around for any sign of Jessicana before marching home. She didn't feel like shadow tumbling right now because thoughts were swarming her head like a hive of angry bees. She knew it would be a long walk home, so she decided to jog.

Halfway home, she spotted a dark figure hiding behind a tree. A second later it vanished. Chills ran down Roseabelle's spine. She was being followed!

Maybe shadow tumbling was a good idea. She ran into the shadow of a large boulder and closed her eyes. She pictured her house and stomped her foot. She felt her body glide through air and land on the soft dirt. She opened her eyes.

Her amazing home was looming in front of her. Astro liked to call it "the tree palace," and Jessicana's name for it was "the fairy hideout." It was built on six oak trees and was made entirely of wood and thick vegetation. The windows were made out of sea glass, and the door was solid brass. A thick ladder made of vines hung from the door.

Roseabelle leapt onto the ladder and climbed up. She pulled open her door and hurried upstairs. Roseabelle raced along the corridor and flung open the first door on the left, which opened up to her bedroom.

Her walls were light blue and the carpet was leafen grass—a type of Benotripian plant that never withered. Her bed had a silken bedspread and an elegantly carved wooden headboard.

On her twig dresser rested a leafy pouch her mother had given her for her seventh birthday. She still remembered the words Danette had spoken when she had presented the pouch to her. "Never forget that in time of need, this case contains something that will give you great aid. Only open it if I am not here to help."

Roseabelle looked out her window. Danette was probably out in Benotripia somewhere, fulfilling one of her many duties as an honorable ruler. Her mother was not always home, but she promised that her trips would never take longer than two days.

Roseabelle looked at the mango tree leaning against her window. She opened the window and edged herself onto the sill, then jumped onto the tree and sat on a strong limb. She picked a mango and bit into it. Roseabelle wiped the juice that was dribbling off her chin with her hand and gazed out on Benotripia.

From her window she could see Bright Shore Beach. If you took a boat and rode for a long time, you would eventually get to Darvonia. Roseabelle took another bite of mango.

Where was Astro? Training would be about over by now. Was Jessicana okay? Had she found something about Asteran? Her thoughts were interrupted by a scream that came from the beach. "Roseabelle, help! Help—"

The shout was cut off. Roseabelle couldn't see who had made the noise, but that didn't stop her from jumping off the tree and sprinting to Bright Shore Beach. There was no one in sight. Who had screamed, then? She squinted out to the ocean. Not even the smallest boat was out there. Her heart was beating three times faster than usual. The voice had been familiar. Who was it?

The undergrowth that signaled the entrance of Frogipani Jungle rustled a bit. Curious, Roseabelle bent to it and pushed back some foliage to see inside. No one. *Well*, she thought, *it could have been a gold-striped frog.*

Gold-striped frogs were fairly common in Benotripia. They liked to rest in dense places and were quick as an arrow.

"That's probably what it was," Roseabelle tried to convince herself. But then if that had been the situation, who screamed?

Confusion filled her mind. She wished that Astro would come soon.

Roseabelle looked at her home. She walked back to the mango tree, climbed it, and hoisted herself up into her room. Roseabelle skittered downstairs and looked out the kitchen window. Outside sat a parrot looking around wildly.

"Jessicana, is that you?" Roseabelle called out.

The parrot squawked excitedly and Roseabelle opened the window so her friend could fly through.

In a split second a blonde-haired girl stood in the parrot's place, clutching a rather creased raven feather. "Oh, Roseabelle," she called, sounding relieved. "There you are. I have a bundle of news for you."

"Where's Astro?" Roseabelle asked. Jessicana's face paled.

"He's not with you? I thought training was over," Jessicana said, panicking.

"Don't worry—we'll find him," Roseabelle soothed.

At that moment, a "Look out below!" came from the roof. There was a loud crash and then silence.

"Astro!" Jessicana and Roseabelle cried out at the same time. Roseabelle dashed out the door and leaped upward. Her hands clasped on a panel of wood, and she began to slide down. Roseabelle scraped at the wall, searching for a crack that she could hold on to. There were none and she began to fall. Roseabelle spotted the kitchen windowsill and lunged for it. She missed and started to plummet downward.

She pressed all her weight on the wall, and much to her surprise, her fall was halted. Roseabelle looked up. Astro was dangling from the roof, his hand clutching hers.

"Astro," Roseabelle gasped. "What happened?"

"Save the questions for later," Astro said as he pulled Roseabelle up on the roof. "Roseabelle, something fishy is going on, and I don't like it. I'm a little worried. Okay—make that really worried. I need to tell you something. I saw—" Astro began, but he was cut off by a pineapple soaring through the air straight at him.

He snatched it by the leaves and flung it away. "I—" Astro started again, only to see a jagged piece of silver zooming toward him. He simply grabbed it from the air and pocketed it.

"As I was saying—" the lightning boy tried again, but a porcelain bowl headed toward him. He shot a lightning bolt at the bowl and it shattered.

Astro sighed. "Never mind," he said.

"What was that?" Roseabelle said, gaping.

"Uh, nothing," Astro said conspicuously. "Let's just forget about it, okay?"

Roseabelle studied her friend carefully. Astro looked extremely twitchy and nervous, like he wanted to tell Roseabelle something but couldn't.

"Um, all right," Roseabelle said uncertainly.

"Good," he said.

"How do we get down?" Roseabelle asked.

Astro shook his head. "I was going to ask you," he stated.

"Great," Roseabelle groaned. "This just great."

"Well, can't you shadow tumble or something?" Astro questioned.

"Yes, but you wouldn't be able to," Roseabelle answered.

"You could catch me."

Roseabelle looked at him incredulously. "Yeah, like I could catch you." She chuckled. Then she stopped. "Oh Kinetle's cloak!" she exclaimed. "I guess I could."

Before she knew it, Roseabelle had plunged into a shadow, pictured the brass door, and stomped her foot on the roof. She felt herself glide through the air and then land on the wooden platform next to the door. She climbed down the ladder and took a deep breath.

She knew what Astro wanted her to do, but she

was extremely nervous. It, of course, had to do with her Meta-Mord, being another unusual power: fur beam.

Yes, it often sounded ridiculous—but the power actually came in handy at times. On the underside of her elbow was a sickening yellow spot. When she exposed the spot to the sun, her body would sprout fur. She would become stronger, more muscular, and fearsome.

Roseabelle truly disliked to perform fur beam, but right now she had no choice. Roseabelle twisted the spot to the sun and watched as a beam of light hit it. She felt herself twist upward and grow taller. She saw strands of brown hair grow on her arms and she hoped that no one besides Astro and Jessicana were watching. Her whole body ached, but Roseabelle just gritted her teeth—which had now grown a little longer. Roseabelle looked down at her legs. She was hairy!

"Astro," she growled. "Jump!" The boy jumped from the roof and Roseabelle caught him with her now large hands. He gave a lopsided grin.

"I thought I would never see you like this," he said as he gave a mock sigh. In return, Roseabelle set Astro down and revealed her furry elbow in the sun. She felt her fur, teeth, and body shrink back to their normal size.

A few minutes later, Roseabelle was completely normal. "Whew," she said. "I'm glad that's over."

Astro bit his lip, obviously trying not to laugh.

"Hey, you guys, come on up! We have some matters to discuss," Jessicana called from above.

Roseabelle climbed up the ladder and reentered her home. Astro followed. When they were all inside, sitting at the bark-made table, Jessicana spoke up.

"After I left you, I traced Asteran through Benotripia. He made some interesting stops. He traveled into Bird Song Jungle. There was a little wooden shack next to a palm tree, and he slipped inside. I followed him. It led to an old bar that served a lot of delicacies like coconut soufflé and banana cream pie.

"I was a little amazed by the special treats when the pub was in the middle of the jungle and totally run-down. Asteran sat down and ordered some food. He ate it both exuberantly and hastily.

"After he paid the bartender with a few bronze had-hadile coins, he set off.

"Asteran wound through the jungle and took a shortcut I had never noticed before. It led out of Bird Song and to a dirt path. He walked with quick steps to a small clearing with a large boulder. He trotted out, and I went after him. But the clearing led back to the dense underbrush.

"I searched and searched, but I couldn't find him. I checked back in the clearing—even behind the boulder—but it seemed like he had disappeared. I went through the underbrush nevertheless and found myself on Bright Shore Beach. There was no sign of him. Disappointed, I went to your house and waited on the branch, and here I am!"

"Nice adventure, Jessicana, but may I ask, what's with the raven feather?" Astro questioned.

"Well, while I was tracking Asteran, this fell out of his pocket," Jessicana answered.

"Can I have a look?" Roseabelle asked. Jessicana handed the feather to her. Roseabelle took it. She quietly pored over it with great care. When she felt the middle of it, she cringed and moaned. Her entire body went rigid, and Jessicana watched in horror as Roseabelle squirmed out of her seat and fell to the floor.

CHAPTER 3
The Dreamworld

"W HAT'S GOING ON?" JESSICANA CRIED. Astro leapt to Roseabelle's side and saw that she was clutching the feather tightly. His eyes quivered with fear, and he reached for the feather. Roseabelle rolled over.

Astro tried to snatch it a second time, but Roseabelle violently kicked her legs in the air. Her eyes were now closed and she was completely out of control. "Kinetle," she groaned. "Kinetle."

When Roseabelle touched the center of the raven feather, she instantly felt nauseated. Her head was light, and she had only the slightest idea of her surroundings. She saw Jessicana's expression turn fearful, and felt herself slip and land with a thud. She tried to get back up, but she didn't have the strength. Roseabelle was beginning to black out now. The last thing she saw was Astro bending over, his eyes full of concern.

"Who's Kinetle?" Jessicana wondered out loud.

"I don't know," Astro replied, still struggling to get the feather.

"Darvonians, Darvonians," Roseabelle muttered. "Darvonians."

"Did you hear that?" Astro asked as he lunged on top of Roseabelle to get the feather. Jessicana nodded. "Well, if we're ever going to get this feather out her hand, you're going to need to help," Astro said.

Jessicana bent down and said, "I have an idea." She whispered something in Roseabelle's ear. Roseabelle paused for a moment, giving Astro the opportunity to grab the feather from her. Roseabelle began to open her eyes.

Something aroused Roseabelle from her faint. She was lying on the ground on a rocky shore. By the looks of it, the land did not seem to match up with Benotripia. There were many mountains, caves, boulders, and pieces of sharp rock. A figure with a black cloak strode to her. "Rise," a harsh voice commanded.

Roseabelle struggled to her feet. "Have you got her?" the figure asked.

Roseabelle was confused. "Um, what do you mean?" she asked.

The man took in a quick breath. "Imposter!" he bellowed. "Do you not know who I am?" Roseabelle, a bit frightened, shook her head boldly.

"I am Ugagush, son of Kinetle, and leader of the Darvonians!" Ugagush shouted. "And you will not escape. Never shall you leave this state."

Kinetle? Roseabelle had heard about her. She was merciless, greedy, and cruel. Her son must be equally so. Roseabelle had to get free.

She turned to run, but an invisible wall blocked her. She heard Ugagush howling with laughter.

Suddenly she heard a voice: "Roseabelle you are in the dream world. Don't worry—we're coming." It was Jessicana's voice. Roseabelle was comforted, and she stopped struggling and trying to run.

Then everything began to black out again. The last image before she became unconscious was Ugagush shrieking, "*Noooo!*"

Roseabelle sat up. She was back in her house with Astro and Jessicana kneeling beside her. "Whoa," she muttered. "That was weird."

"Roseabelle!" Jessicana cried out. She embraced her friend. "What in the name of Danette happened?"

Roseabelle told them all about the sensation with the feather, what happened, who she saw, and how she ended up back here.

"I'll say that is quite an adventure," Jessicana remarked.

"Jessicana, what were you talking about when you said the 'dream world'?" Roseabelle asked.

Jessicana's expression turned grave. "Roseabelle," she said, her tone quavering. "It's an ancient myth. Before I didn't believe in it, but now I do. According to the legend, the dream world was created by an IB."

"What's an IB?" Astro asked.

"IB stands for *Imitation Benotripian*," Jessicana answered steadily. "And they are as rare as Meta-Mords. They are born into the Darvonian race, but they look nothing like their parents and could easily pass for a Benotripian. IBs are very intelligent, and so far, none of them have been on the good side."

Astro and Roseabelle were staring at her openly. "How in Benotripia's Beauty do you know all this?" Roseabelle asked her.

Jessicana blushed and shrugged. "Just research in the library, I guess. Anyway," she continued, "the dream world was a sort of place where Darvonians communicated with their own kind. They also trapped Benotripians into a terrible motionless state."

Jessicana paused, waiting for a reaction. Astro was looking eager for her to go on, but Roseabelle was sitting on her chair, keeping her gaze on the floor. "Roseabelle, what's wrong?" Jessicana asked.

Wordlessly, Roseabelle went to the door. She

traveled down the ladder and walked as if in a trance to Bright Shore Beach. Astro and Jessicana shared a look and then scrambled after her. At the beach, Roseabelle squatted down and touched the flower that she had pushed back earlier.

She pushed it back again and called, "You guys, over here!" Astro and Jessicana came to her. "When you were gone this afternoon, I heard a scream. It sounded familiar, but now I know exactly who it was. My mother is in trouble. I came to the beach and checked the bushes. Stay here. I'm going to see again," Roseabelle said.

Astro looked worried as did Jessicana. Jessicana put an arm on Roseabelle's shoulder. We're coming with you," she said firmly.

Without another sound, the threesome crept into the bushes. It was dense, and Roseabelle could barely see. She tried hard not to stumble blindly. When they had gone a long distance, Roseabelle stopped in her tracks.

In front of the auburn-haired girl were footprints. Three pairs, in fact. One was sleek and elegant, one was heavy and clumsy, and the other was thin and long. Roseabelle studied the sleek pair. It seemed like those footprints were uneven, as if the person they belonged to had been dragged.

The footprints continued for a few short paces, then vanished. The other footprints kept going. Roseabelle noticed apricot juice dripping from a leaf. She picked up the leaf, and her eyes widened. She nudged Astro and

Jessicana. "Look," she whispered. It was an intricate, delicate message written in apricot juice!

"Read it," Astro urged. Roseabelle cleared her throat, then, "*Help! This is Danette, leader of the Benotripians. The Darvonians have kidnapped me, and I don't know where they are taking me. If you are reading this, warn my people and tell them to prepare for the enemy's invasion. Do not come after me. Tell my daughter, Roseabelle, to look inside the place where only she will know what I mean. Remember what I say. Tell Roseabelle that Shelby is a—*" Roseabelle read. "It stops there," she said quietly.

No one spoke for a while. Finally Jessicana broke the quiet aura in the trees. "Danette kidnapped? This isn't good, Roseabelle. We have to do something. What does she mean *the place where only she will know what I mean?* It could help us."

Roseabelle didn't reply.

"A—are you all right, Roseabelle?" Astro asked. Roseabelle lifted up her face.

Tears were dripping from her eyes. She hastily rubbed her face on her sleeve and turned to the beach. "Astro, Jessicana, the thing that she wants me to know. It's at my house. Let's go."

CHAPTER 4

Fight for the Pouch

WHEN THEY ARRIVED BACK AT HER HOUSE, Roseabelle leapt up the ladder and opened the door. She ran in the house, up the stairs, and into her room.

On her dresser was the little leaf pouch Danette had given her. She grabbed it and jogged back downstairs. Roseabelle scampered on the sand back to her friends and showed Astro and Jessicana.

"Open it," Astro said.

Roseabelle was about to lift the green flap when a deep voice growled "Stop right there." The three friends whirled around.

Three figures in black robes were standing in front of them, armed with different weapons. One beefy man held a trapita, a long rod with three sharp blades on the sides. One man bore a thepgile, a round disk with spikes on the edges and a wire attached to the middle. The other end of the wire could be clipped on your wrist. The last figure looked female. The figure was clearly the leader and was clutching a dragocone ray.

Dragocone rays were part fire, part sunlight, and part magic. If you got hit by one, you would be knocked down with the force of a wild animal and experience some painful burns. The only substance they didn't affect were silk and latick, a kind of precious metal. You had to wear silk gloves to safely hold the weapon.

The third figure was wearing silk gloves. "Darvonians," Roseabelle whispered.

"Hand over the pouch," the first man commanded.

"Umm, let me think about that," Astro said. "How about this: no way."

It happened so fast that Roseabelle and her friends didn't even see the Darvonians coming.

The Darvonian with the dragocone ray swung her ray and charged the three friends. The other two figures went after her.

Roseabelle's first instinct was to use one of her powers. But which one?

She turned to look at her friends. Jessicana was still, her face pale. Astro was like stone for one second, then just as the dark ones closed in, Astro lifted a finger, and a sharp lightning bolt erupted from it.

It knocked into the cloaked man with the trapita

and sent him flying. The other uninjured figures didn't pause for a second.

The Darvonian with the dragocone ray reached Roseabelle first. She tried to snatch the pouch, but Roseabelle quickly dove under her arm and backed away. The Darvonian headed for her again, this time raising her dragocone ray.

Roseabelle remembered the dark figure with the thepgile and whirled around just in time to see the weapon spin right to her. Roseabelle sidestepped it and yanked the wire where it was attached to the deadly weapon. Her movement sent the thepgile zooming into a tree trunk.

Roseabelle quickly turned back to face the sinister figure. She was just in time, for the Darvonian had just wound her ray and the weapon was inches away from her arm that held the pouch.

Roseabelle immediately decided that now was the time to use some of her powers. She turned to the trapita that the Darvonian had been holding. It now lay untouched beside the large man. Using one of her more common powers, Roseabelle performed telekinesis. In a quarter of a second, Roseabelle lifted the weapon with her mind and levitated it into her waiting hand.

Roseabelle turned to block the ray. She was in time to stop the ray from hitting the pouch, but she couldn't stop it from hitting herself. The ray hit her shoulder instead, and Roseabelle was sent tumbling right into

Jessicana. The blow was so great that Roseabelle lost part of her vision for several moments.

She saw Astro shooting lightning bolts at the two figures before them. Since the man was so large, the bolt hit him easily, but the leader was a more difficult target. Astro shot bolt after bolt, and finally one of the lightning bolts hit the third figure's arm.

The now-crippled Darvonian cried out in anguish and the ray flew out of the third's hand. Roseabelle was able to stand. She ran to the ray and took the third's gloves and slid them onto her own hands. She picked up the ray and turned to the third trespasser.

"Besides the fact that there are multiple Benotripian homes in close range that I can signal for help, you and your men are injured. I can assure you that Benotripians will not tolerate your presence here. Go while you still have the chance. Leave."

The figure gave her a piercing, withering, defeated look. The leader growled. Roseabelle looked the dark Darvonian in the eye.

"Go," she commanded.

The Darvonian made a series of grunts and growls, then stood and pulled her henchman up with her good arm. Together they limped to the beach.

"Jessicana, make sure they leave, will you?" Roseabelle asked. Jessicana transformed into a parrot and flew off.

"That was generous," Astro commented.

"Astro," she replied, "they're our ticket to reach Darvonia. They probably need to get a boat, right? I suspect they got here on a one-way trip. Perhaps the pouch provides transportation. Anyway, they'll have to build or take a boat. Either will take some time. We open the pouch, get prepared, and go after my mother."

Astro nodded. "Good idea," he said. A minute later, Jessicana returned in her human form.

"They're at the beach, all right," she said. "And they are starting to make a tiny raft. According to my judgment, they should be finished in two days."

"Good," Roseabelle said lightly. "But now let's go into my home and open the pouch." Together the three friends boarded the rope ladder. The sun was beginning to set and they sat at the kitchen table.

Astro eyed the pouch. "Your honor," he said. Roseabelle took a deep breath and lifted the green flap. She reached inside and pulled out a withered piece of trutan—a parchment-like substance that Benotripians used for writing. The house was quiet.

"I-is that it?" Jessicana asked, looking at the trutan.

"I don't know," Astro replied, his voice unbelieving. It appeared blank, but there was something unusual about it.

"It's almost dusk, you guys," Roseabelle said. "So why don't you go to your homes and get some sleep?"

Jessicana shivered. "My parents are on vacation on the north side. I don't want to go to the house alone.

Can I spend the night with you?" Jessicana asked with hope.

Roseabelle nodded.

"Uh, yeah about that, Roseabelle, as you know my dad is busy with his job and everything, and, well, my mom is on a cruise, so could I stay too?" Astro asked. Astro's father worked for *The Tropical Times* and was usually all over Benotripia doing what a reporter does.

Roseabelle sighed. "I guess so," she said. Astro let out a whoop.

"All right, where do I sleep?" Astro and Jessicana asked at the same time. Roseabelle thought for a moment. Her home had six rooms. Downstairs was the kitchen. Upstairs was her room, Danette's room, the guest room (it had once been Magford's "working room"), Danette's study, and the tower room—they called it—which was sort of a mini library.

"Jessicana, you can stay in the tower room. It has lots of books, so I think you'll be happy there. Astro, I think the guest room will suit you," Roseabelle offered.

Jessicana and Astro bobbed their heads and hurried up the stairs. She turned back to the parchment. She then walked up the stairs and went to her mother's study.

She sat down at the large desk. Roseabelle took a small bottle of ink made out of papaya juice. She randomly doodled a raft on the trutan, and then after finding some blankets and pillowcases in the laundry for her friends, she trekked to her room.

She laid the trutan on her dresser and climbed into bed. She closed her tired eyes, not noticing something expanding from the trutan.

CHAPTER 5

Midnight Raft

ROSEABELLE WOKE UP AND YAWNED. WAS IT time for training yet? Any minute Danette would call her down for breakfast, urging her not to be late.

But then Roseabelle remembered. Her mother had been kidnapped! The pouch—the trutan! Roseabelle turned over to her dresser and shrieked. "Astro, Jessicana!" she shouted. "You have got to see this!"

On her very own dresser sat a long wooden raft. It was made out of tree trunks lashed together with bamboo. Roseabelle swore that if she laid horizontally on the craft, it would take five of her to cover all of it. Jessicana came in, then Astro.

"How did that get there?" Jessicana sputtered.

Roseabelle picked up the trutan that she had drawn

on last night. There was not a spot of ink to be found.

"No way," she murmured. She turned to her friends. "Guys," she said. "I drew a picture of a raft, and a raft came out of the trutan! This is no ordinary trutan, for sure. It's an extraordinary gift."

"Whoa," muttered Jessicana.

"Cool," Astro said enthusiastically.

Roseabelle sighed. "I think we should prepare today. Astro, scout from the beach. If those troublesome Darvonians come back or if you see a ship on the horizon, let me know right away."

"Got it," he said.

"Jessicana, go to your house and bring me two mottels. Loyal ones," Roseabelle instructed.

"I'll be back," she said.

"I'll stay here and *pack*. More like draw. Anyway, let's plan to leave tomorrow," Roseabelle said. Jessicana transformed into a bird and flew out the window. Astro went out the door, climbed down the ladder, and set off for the beach.

Roseabelle turned back to the trutan. She went up to Danette's study and drew three large backpacks complete with ice coolers, water bottles, solar hand warmers, dragocone rays in silk bags, and, for some strange reason, potted plants.

Roseabelle decided to get a snack. She poured herself some water and ate a banana. She then went to her room and pulled on jeans and a green T-shirt.

When she went back to her mother's study, the backpacks were already starting to form. She looked out the window and saw Jessicana running to the house, followed by two gentle-looking mottels. One mottel was brown with black specks in its feathers while the other one had white and black stripes.

The two mottels flew through the window while Jessicana raced to the ladder and entered through the door. "Got them?" Roseabelle asked.

Jessicana nodded, breathless.

"I hope Astro's holding up with those Darvonians," Roseabelle said.

"Me too."

"Follow me," Roseabelle invited. She showed Jessicana the trutan. The top half of the backpacks were protruding from it. "Jessicana, after they're fully formed, could you strap them onto the raft?" Roseabelle asked.

"I could do that," Jessicana said. They waited for about an hour, spending it by reading about Darvonia in the tower room, something Jessicana thoroughly enjoyed.

She has always been the smart one, Roseabelle thought.

Afterward, Roseabelle went to check on the backpacks. "They're ready," she announced to Jessicana.

The parrot girl found straps on the raft and clasped them around the backpacks. Meanwhile, Roseabelle drew a pile of blankets and other supplies. *Well, we do have to be prepared*, Roseabelle thought.

As Roseabelle picked up her book from the tower room, she read, "The government of Darvonia is uncertain. Kinetle is the leader. Her husband, as far as we can tell, is either dead or lost. She has seven children: two twins about twenty-five, a twenty-year-old son, a seventeen-year-old daughter, a fourteen-year-old son, an eleven-year-old son, and a young daughter of age four. It is rumored that one of these children is an IB."

"An IB?" Roseabelle said out loud. This was not good news. She recalled someone following her from school. Could that person be a spy for Darvonia?

When the supplies were done, Roseabelle carried them to Jessicana. The blonde girl placed them in the packs. Roseabelle took a few books from the tower room and put them in the backpacks. She drew oars on the trutan and waited.

Jessicana came to her. "You can go to bed, Roseabelle. I'll send a message to Astro," she said. Sleep sounded refreshing, so Roseabelle went up to her room and collapsed onto the bed.

CHAPTER 6

Sea Voyage

ROSEABELLE, WAKE UP! IT'S TIME. THE Darvonians are leaving. I packed clothes and food and the trutan. Let's go!"

Roseabelle opened her eyes. Jessicana was standing above her dressed in a slender blue wrap dress and a gray jacket. "I'm coming," Roseabelle sleepily muttered.

She stood and, when Jessicana left the room, dressed in a peach shirt with sleeves that went down to her elbows, light orange leggings, and pale sandals.

Roseabelle took two small bottles of cherry ink from her dresser in case they ran out. She wanted to make certain the trutan was accessible.

Roseabelle slipped a small sparkling ruby pendant into her pocket for good luck.

When she went downstairs, Jessicana was at the

front door in parrot form. "Follow," she squawked.

Jessicana flew to the beach and Roseabelle ran after her. Astro was standing at the beach, the raft next to him. The two mottels were sitting beside him. "Hurry," he said. "We're losing them."

He pointed to the sea where a small raft was holding up three figures. Jessicana turned back into a girl and they scrambled onto the raft. The mottels fluttered and landed on the watercraft.

"I'll paddle," Jessicana offered.

"Me too," Roseabelle said.

Each girl took an oar and started to row. It was tiring and Roseabelle's muscles were sore, but still she pushed on.

"I'll take Jessicana's place," Astro said. He took hold of an oar. They made sure that they didn't lose sight of the Darvonians. They pushed on and on.

Jessicana switched places, and Roseabelle, relieved, let go. At noon Roseabelle pulled out a canteen of coconut juice. She handed some to Astro and Jessicana, then drank some herself. It began to get extremely windy.

"Roseabelle," Jessicana said. "Could you make a sail? The trutan is in my backpack." Roseabelle pulled it out and took some cherry ink from her pack. She drew a pole with a sail attached.

The lines started to get bolder, and Roseabelle said, "I'll row for you, Astro. Watch the trutan."

She took hold of an oar and pushed. She thought

about her powers. There was one power that wasn't as unusual as her others. She could transform into a dolphin. It might really come in handy. She had a feeling this was going to be a long trip and doubted that it would be windy the entire time.

She kept pushing and pulling, pushing and pulling.

Soon Astro took Jessicana's place. The sky turned to dusk. She was grateful when Jessicana took her load.

It was windier than ever, so she checked on the sail. It was ready! She hoisted it up, and Astro and Jessicana stopped rowing. The raft picked up speed.

Roseabelle pulled out three mangos from a backpack and handed two to Jessicana and Astro. She ate one herself then dug out some water from her pack and passed it around. They decided that one should keep watch during the night and make sure that they were in range of the Darvonians.

They pulled out two blankets. Jessicana would keep first watch. Roseabelle sat back against her blanket and quickly fell asleep.

"Roseabelle, you have last watch," Astro whispered. Roseabelle's eyes opened. She gave her blanket to Astro and went to the front of the raft. The raft was losing speed; the wind was dying down. She took down the sail and then checked in her backpack for rope. There it was. She tied it around her waist, then attached one end of the rope to one side of the raft and the other end to the other side.

Roseabelle took a deep breath and jumped into the water. She pictured a dolphin in her mind, and when she glanced down at her body, it was smooth and slippery. She flicked her tail, and Roseabelle and the raft sped on. Roseabelle swam on and on as fast as she could.

As dawn approached, Astro and Jessicana began to stir. She heard a deep sleepy voice: "Where's Roseabelle?"

This time another voice, "Here, silly—" The voice cut off. "Where is she? Astro, this isn't a joke!"

"Hey, I asked you first."

"Astro, this isn't funny. Are you hiding her?"

"Sure I'm hiding her. Whatever! How could I hide her on this open raft?"

"Do you think she went overboard?"

"Hey, why is the sail down?"

"Who cares about the sail?"

"Why are we going so fast?"

"I don't know, I—"

Just then Roseabelle let out a squeal. Both Astro and Jessicana looked down at the dolphin.

"Roseabelle?" Jessicana asked. Roseabelle thought hard of her human form and then changed. She grinned up at Jessicana, the rope still clinging to her waist.

"That's me." Roseabelle laughed.

"Seriously, what were you trying to do? Scare us?" Jessicana scolded.

"No, the wind was dying down, so I transformed to speed us up," Roseabelle said.

Astro laughed. "You never told us you could turn into a dolphin." He chuckled. "This is totally great!"

"Well," Jessicana admitted. "It is pretty fortunate. Good thinking!"

Roseabelle grinned. "Well, we had better not lose those Darvonians," she cried out. Roseabelle dived back into the ocean and thought of how good the water felt on her. Without even realizing it, Roseabelle transformed and began to swim forward.

Roseabelle swam for a while, but when the Darvonians stopped, Jessicana told Roseabelle to have lunch. Astro and Jessicana would row. Roseabelle transformed and pulled herself out of the water. Jessicana found a long cloth that served as a towel and handed it to Roseabelle, who dried herself off.

Roseabelle discovered a few oranges, and she ate them hungrily. She thought that they should have enough food and water for another couple of days. Soon they would have to break out the trutan. Roseabelle untied the rope and stuck it in her pack. She pulled a blanket from the raft, curled up, and caught a few hours of sleep.

CHAPTER 7

Scythterrian

ASTRO ROWED ON WITH JESSICANA BY HIS SIDE. They were keeping up a good pace, but the Darvonians were starting to disappear into a thick fog ahead of them. It wasn't any ordinary fog either. There was something mystical—something mysterious—about it.

"Wake Roseabelle up," Jessicana urged. Astro reluctantly put his oar on the raft and shook Roseabelle gently. She sat up and rubbed her eyes.

"Oar duty?" Roseabelle asked sleepily.

"No," Jessicana said. "But you have to have a look at this."

"Hold on a minute," Roseabelle said. She peered ahead. "Strange," she muttered. She reached inside her backpack and pulled out a thick scroll titled *The Known*

Secrets of Darvonia. She unrolled it to the table of contents and scanned the page. "There it is!" Roseabelle exclaimed.

She traced her finger on "Travails of Darvonia." She then unrolled to the chapter. She read, *"Only spies for Benotripia know this important information."* It listed a bunch of coordinates and directions that, to Roseabelle, were meaningless. Roseabelle continued: *"On the way there stands a thick fog. You have to go straight through it. Do not try to avoid it, for such could get you lost. It is there for a reason."* Roseabelle and Astro looked at Jessicana.

"Go straight through," they chimed together.

"I would if one of you would row with me," Jessicana said.

Roseabelle took the oar and rowed as hard as she could. A current was tilting them sideways. She and Jessicana struggled against it, but it was too strong.

"Help us, Astro," the girls cried out as the raft nearly capsized. Astro fastened his grip to Roseabelle's oar. Together they pushed and pushed, but it was no use. The current was taking them away altogether.

"Here," Roseabelle said. "Stay here." She took the rope from her pack and tied it around her waist. Then without another word, she plunged into the icy cold water. Astro and Jessicana looked around wildly, and they pushed and pulled with the oars. They were both thinking the same thing. "Hurry, Roseabelle!"

Roseabelle pictured the smooth texture of a dolphin.

When she looked at her hands, they were no longer hands. Flippers had taken their place. She propelled her tail forward and only forward. She tried to balance herself out, shifting right then left. It was working! The raft was floating forward slowly but surely. With the current it was hard work. Roseabelle gracefully swished her tail back and forth.

When they got past the current, she sighed with relief. She pictured her human form, and in a minute she could no longer hold her breath underwater very long. She rose to the surface and put her hands on the raft.

She boosted herself onboard and then removed the rope. As soon as she got on, her friends cheered and almost upset the raft by jumping up and down. Now that they had entered the fog, they could hardly see anything. The white mist curled around their feet as Jessicana and Astro rowed through.

Roseabelle was busy reading the chapter "Travails of Darvonia." She read quietly, "*Once past the mist, you will enter Blackwater Sea (which is actually an ocean). These waters are the most dangerous you will ever enter. Sea monsters lurk beneath the murky waves, seeking their next meal, and carnivorous fish bite into water-born crafts, causing them to sink.*"

Roseabelle shuddered. She put the scroll away and was about to tell her friends when their craft broke through the fog. Roseabelle's heart sank. They were in Blackwater Sea.

It was the scariest thing Roseabelle had ever seen. The black waters churned and bounced up and down. Waste and garbage littered the surface, and she heard Jessicana yelp.

Roseabelle thought about doing just that. She saw the Darvonians up ahead sailing smoothly along. Then the Darvonians' craft stopped. Since the sun was beginning to set, Roseabelle decided to stop too.

"Let's get some sleep," she advised. She curled up on her blanket. Astro took watch. Within a few minutes, Roseabelle was temporarily dead to the world.

* * * * *

Violent rocking of the raft woke Roseabelle up. She looked around. No one was on watch! Jessicana and Astro were both snoring away. Roseabelle peered in the distance. Not a craft in sight. The Darvonians! Where were they? She shook her friends awake.

"Wake up," she hissed. They sat up. "Who fell asleep during their watch? The Darvonians are gone."

Astro turned bright red. "Er, sorry," he said.

"Sorry?" Jessicana bellowed. "Sorry! Is that all you can say? We've lost the Darvonians and have the tiniest, slimmest chance of finding Roseabelle's mom. It's all your fault, and all you can say is sorry? Come on!"

"Roseabelle, Jessicana, I'm really sorry," he said.

Roseabelle sighed. Astro looked distraught. "It's okay, Astro," she said.

She tugged on her oar and started to row. Astro took the other one. They moved in silence, secretly debating which direction they should head. Suddenly Jessicana sat up straight.

"What's that noise?" she asked uneasily.

Astro and Roseabelle shared a look. "Are you okay? I don't hear anything," Roseabelle stated.

"Did you hit your head?" Astro joked.

"No seriously, the water's vibrating."

Roseabelle hated to admit it, but now she felt it too. "Guys," she asked. "What's going—"

A huge bellow came from the water, and a monstrous shape erupted from the icy depths. A wave the size of a tsunami swept the raft to the sky. They all screamed.

The raft smacked against the water, and then Roseabelle realized what was happening.

It was a sea monster—as tall as five stockfish (a type of fish as big as a blue whale). It had sickly green scales with a yellowish tint, two crests on its bumpy head, sharp claws, a mouth full of teeth—just one tooth was the length of Roseabelle from her shoes to her hair— and a terrible tail. The tail was long and covered with spikes and at the very end was a nasty point hiding beneath layers of giant needles.

From her short research, Roseabelle recognized it immediately. "Scythterrian," she whispered. The three friends were paralyzed with fear. The monster began to strike again. It lifted its tail, and then, quick as a flash, it came at them. Roseabelle saw it in slow motion.

Jessicana screamed for the second time and pointed to her backpack. Somehow Roseabelle understood. She zipped it open and found a silk bag. She tore it open. Inside was the dragocone ray. Next to that lay a pair of silk gloves. Roseabelle knew what Jessicana wanted her to do.

She pulled on the gloves and grabbed the ray. The tail was hurtling toward her at the speed of lightning. She raised the ray and—*thwack*—the monster went flying. It catapulted into the air and then plummeted back down again. "Look out!" Astro called.

They dove underwater just in time. It was chaos. The impact made thousands of tons of water fly everywhere. The Scythterrian might've hit the bottom of the ocean because a giant whirlpool begun, and everything was being sucked into it, including the raft, which was right next to them.

They struggled with the raft, but when it started to drag them underwater, they let it go. Roseabelle suddenly had an idea. "Get on," she instructed.

She handed the gloves and the ray to Jessicana and jumped into the water. Roseabelle soon transformed into a magnificent dolphin. She pulled the craft, but the whirlpool was still hanging on to it. She needed help. Desperate help. She looked down and saw the Scythterrian.

Its deep, meaty mouth was hanging open, ready to

catch his prey. *Well, all right then*, she thought. *If I can't get out, I'll have to go in.*

She transformed back to human and let the whirlpool pull them in. The three friends held their breath as the raft pulled them under the surface of the water. The Scythterrian looked triumphant. The raft dragged down and down, faster and faster. The craft got so close to the monster's mouth that Roseabelle could practically reach out and touch one of the sharp teeth. Astro closed his eyes. A string of bubbles escaped from Jessicana's mouth that could have been a whimper.

Roseabelle grabbed the ray from Jessicana and swung it, hitting the Scythterrian's tooth. This time the blow was weaker, but the sea monster was pushed back all the same.

Wow, Roseabelle thought. *He must be strong. Two blows with a ray are usually deadly.*

This time the Scythterrian couldn't recover. It lay motionless on the ocean floor. Roseabelle dragged the raft and her friends to the surface before taking another gulp of air and diving deep. Roseabelle crept up and climbed up the monster's scaly chest. Its eyes were closed. Doubtfully she leaned over. Its claws snatched at Roseabelle, but she swam up just in time. Gasping for breath, she reached her watercraft and accepted Jessicana's outstretched, pale hand.

Astro started to say, "Is it gone?" when his response came instantly.

The monster rose above the surface of the water, a red glint in its eye. But his tail was spotted with burns, and when it opened its mouth, Roseabelle saw that two of his teeth were missing.

After what had happened, Roseabelle had expected that the monster would be smart enough to back off. Apparently she was wrong. The monster leapt at her so quickly that Roseabelle wasn't prepared.

From behind, Astro pushed her, causing her to free fall into the water. The monster clawed the air where she had been floating and bellowed with rage.

She managed to swim underneath its belly, veering to the side. When Roseabelle got to the side, she carefully hoisted herself up and somehow climbed onto its back. She took her ray and plunged it into the sea monster's scales.

It howled and flew up. It flipped back and forth, and Roseabelle fell off.

She started to plummet down. It was happening so fast. Roseabelle blacked out when she hit the water.

CHAPTER 8
Darvonia

Breathe, Roseabelle, breathe. I hope she's all right."

"Stop fussing, Jessicana. She's waking up."

Roseabelle's eyes fluttered open. Jessicana was in front of her, holding a maroon bottle and a glass spoon filled with a fine peach powder. "You're awake," Jessicana cried. She shoved the contents of the spoon into Roseabelle's mouth. It tasted like orange with a touch of sourness and a sprinkle of saltiness.

When Roseabelle had swallowed, she asked Jessicana frantically, "What happened? Is the monster dead?"

Jessicana nodded. "For good," she said. "You took quite a plunge. Astro swam out there and pulled you back to the raft. I flew and checked to see if the sea creature was dead. I transformed back and landed on his stomach. Nothing happened. I told Astro, and we set sail again." Jessicana paused to feed more powder to Roseabelle. "The wind picked up, and we put up the sail. Soon we saw a small dot in the distance. We caught up, and well, we think it's Darvonia! I know you will go crazy over this, but you've been out for six days."

Roseabelle nearly spit out the medicine. Six days! They had been at sea for more than a week. Roseabelle sat up. Astro was digging in his pack. "We haven't been eating a lot," he explained. "I think this is a good time."

Roseabelle looked around. Sure enough, a dot was in the distance. But now it was less of a dot. It was growing bigger every minute. Astro handed her a handful of honey-covered nuts, which were considered a type of delicacy in Benotripia. Roseabelle downed them quickly.

Jessicana pulled out a handful of hadhadiles, machegh's (black gold coins and a type of currency), and kierteks (white gold coins and the most valuable currency in Benotripia).

"What's that for?" Roseabelle asked. Jessicana shrugged. "Darvonians use precious metals for melting them down and them reforming them into their own currency," Jessicana said. "You never know when you might need a coin."

She put them away and asked if Roseabelle could watch because the sun was setting. Roseabelle nodded. She took a piece of wraptook (a flat bread) from her backpack and began to chew.

Roseabelle was extremely tired, but she had learned her lesson not to fall asleep at this time thanks to Astro. She watched as Darvonia came closer and closer and closer. After eating another loaf of wraptook, she tapped Jessicana and Astro on the shoulder as they began to pull up on the shore.

Roseabelle and Jessicana pulled on the oars. The beach looked deserted, but still they made sure that they were safely hidden from prying eyes. As soon as they reached the shore, Roseabelle gagged. Darvonia was terrible! The land was dirty, dark, and scorched. Tree stumps lay in every direction and trash was everywhere. The land was quite mountainous, so when they dragged the raft on the island, Astro ran off to find a place where they could sleep, while Roseabelle and Jessicana crept off to a boulder for a temporary hiding place.

Astro came back. "There's a cave nearby," he panted. "Come on."

The three friends discreetly hiked up the rocky terrain. Astro led them to a small crevice in the rock. It led to a cave. "Perfect," Roseabelle whispered.

She set the raft down along with their other belongings. "Someone will need to guard this at all times. We can switch," Roseabelle stated.

Astro and Jessicana nodded. "Also," Jessicana piped up, "we need to be ready for a hasty exit. Let's not unpack entirely."

The others agreed, and then they began to set up

camp. Jessicana laid two blankets down, and Astro set out the hand warmers. "I'm going to check out Darvonia," Roseabelle said.

Astro shuddered. "Be careful," he said.

"I will," Roseabelle replied.

She crept out of the cave and set off.

Once Roseabelle was back on the shore, she started off into Darvonia. It was a long walk. She didn't see any Darvonians. Then she heard some commotion.

Roseabelle crept along stealthily. She looked ahead. There was a high metal gate that joined a stone wall. The wall wrapped around a large area. Roseabelle figured it must be a village. She looked at the gates. They were firmly padlocked. She looked at the wall. It was several feet high.

Roseabelle put her hands on the wall. It was jagged and rocky and had many places where she could find holds for her hands and feet. She began to climb. It was difficult work. Roseabelle knew that if she fell, well, she didn't want to think about it.

When she was at the top, she peered cautiously over the side. It was a village. At the front were two guards making sure no outsiders got in. *It's a clever strategy,* Roseabelle thought. *It appears on the outside as if someone could climb over the gates and just walk in.* Sadly that wasn't the case.

Further off was a large campfire. Young girls were

dancing around it using their hands to show expression. All of them had ghostly skin and dark hair. The black marks behind their ears signaled their own culture mark. Beyond the campfire were many huts constructed of mud and burnt wood. The houses kept going and going, then stopped at a large building. Two guards with solemn faces were standing in front of it, one armed with a long sword and shield and the other with a brutal thepgile. She considered climbing to find out why they were guarding it when the girls stopped dancing and bowed.

"Archery," a male voice called. The boys pulled out bows and quivers of arrows and aimed for the wall. Roseabelle ducked down and hoped that they hadn't seen her. She carefully scaled down the wall and ran off. She couldn't help thinking about the building. When she got to the rocks, she began to climb. Finally she reached the cave. Jessicana and Astro looked up, their faces shining.

"What did you find?" Astro asked. Roseabelle told them about the village and the events that had occurred. After silence, Jessicana spoke.

"Do you think that's where your mom is, Roseabelle?"

Roseabelle pondered it for a moment.

"Perhaps," she decided.

"The sun," Astro said promptly, "is going down. I suggest we eat and then get some sleep. Since Roseabelle went on that expedition, she can give out the watch schedule for tonight."

They all looked at Roseabelle. "Jessicana, you watch till about midnight. I will guard until four in the morning. Astro, you'll watch till eight." Roseabelle said.

They all nodded. Jessicana took a knife encrusted with pearls from her bag and went to the front entrance. Roseabelle lay down on her blanket. It was harshly cold, so she put on her hand warmer.

She could hear Astro snoring next to her. She desperately needed some sleep. It was all such a shock to her.

She recalled her mother's message they had found. The last part was *"Tell my daughter Roseabelle that her trainer Shelby is a"* and then it had cut off. What was Shelby? Was she truly a Benotripian? But she couldn't possibly be a Darvonian! She bore no resemblance to one. Her tired state called her soon to a deep sleep.

Jessicana shook her awake at midnight. Roseabelle sat up. Jessicana whispered softly in ear that she couldn't use the dragocone ray because it might attract attention.

"I have some weapons in my bag," Jessicana whispered, "so take your pick."

Roseabelle gave her blanket to Jessicana and then reached inside her friend's bag. Next to the ray was a trapita and two rusty thepgiles. Roseabelle wasn't the expert at thepgiles, so she settled with the trapita.

Seizing it, she walked out and readied her weapon. The trees rustled, but no one came.

Four hours later, Roseabelle was about to get Astro when a dark shape streaked across the rocks. Roseabelle gasped and readied herself, drawing into the shadows. Not a peep. Sighing and assuring herself it was probably her imagination, she tapped Astro on the shoulder.

He woke up, and Roseabelle motioned for Astro to choose a weapon. She set down the arrows in Jessicana's bag and then curled up on a blanket.

CHAPTER 9

Distraction

"LET'S GET GOING," ASTRO SAID IN HER EAR. Roseabelle shot up and bolted from the cave floor. She changed into a green long-sleeved shirt and a pair of green and brown pants with leather boots.

After her friends were ready to go, Roseabelle led them down and to the village. When they got there, it was quiet. Astro boosted Roseabelle up to the wall.

The campfire was gone, but the cloaked guards were still at the gates and in front of the building. "We have to get in there," Roseabelle reasoned, "but how?"

"Wait here," Astro whispered. "Give me a boost, Jessicana."

When Astro was up, he winked and scampered away. Jessicana and Roseabelle shared a look and rolled their eyes.

On the far side of the wall, Astro took a deep breath and then whistled. He ducked.

The cloaksman looked at where Astro had been and frowned. "Who's there?" he growled. He stalked over to the wall. Astro flattened himself against it. The cloaksman shrugged and walked away. *Not the brightest of guards*, Roseabelle thought.

Then Astro whistled again.

"Who goes there?" the cloaksman roared. He stalked over again, his face contorted with confusion.

Astro snatched a spare robe from the ground and pulled a hammer from his backpack, which was on his back. He banged the top with the hammer, hoping to attract attention. The cloaksman marched closer.

Astro banged it a second time. The Darvonian was nearly to Astro.

Astro banged it a third time, also accidently releasing a lightning bolt that hit the wall. The top part crumbled. The guard shouted with fury, and Astro pulled the robe on so he could pass for a Darvonian, then fled.

The cloaksman jumped over the now-crumbling structure and chased after him. When the other cloaksman realized what had happened, he also followed after Astro.

"That was brave," Roseabelle said.

"Should we drop down?" Jessicana asked.

Roseabelle nodded. "The other cloaksmen are too far away to see us. Let's make a move before they come back."

Jessicana changed into a parrot and flew down. Roseabelle smiled. Jessicana had it too easy. She took hold of a log protruding upward and clung to it. The weight caused it to come down with a thud. The cloaksman closest to the building watched his perimeter.

Jessicana quickly turned back to her human form and pulled Roseabelle down behind the log. The cloaksman's stare surpassed them. Jessicana breathed a sigh of relief. They stood up and crept around the houses. Roseabelle peeked inside one of the mud-formed windows.

A Darvonian mother was sitting in a burnt wooden chair, carving a wooden sword sheath while three little boys were playing around her feet with a waxy ball. One of the boys stood up, and Jessicana tugged on Roseabelle to continue.

They walked through the village, all the way hoping that no one would spot them. More than a few feet away, the Darvonians were staring straight ahead. The girls were hidden at the side of the building. Roseabelle carefully studied the door. It didn't look locked, but Roseabelle decided she was going to find out what was in the building, locked or not.

She put a hand in front of Jessicana to signal for her to stay put and watched the Darvonians carefully. Roseabelle raced to the back of the building. Once again it was jagged and crooked, so Roseabelle climbed it with ease.

She scaled the mud walls and hoped that the

cloaksmen would be clueless enough to fall for her trap.

Astro was scared. There was no hiding it. The Darvonians were gaining on him, and if they got his hands on him, they would surely realize that he was a Benotripian, not just a troublesome Darvonian kid.

He was getting tired now and didn't know where to go. Running to the cave would lead the guards to it, so he crossed out that idea. Circling around wouldn't be much help. All the weapons were at the cave, so he couldn't fight back.

Astro charged up some rocky land. A cloaksman went after him. He staggered up and up. He then saw a tiny opening in the rock up ahead.

He sprinted using all his energy and turned the corner. He bent down and slid inside. It gave him enough to room to squeeze in. Astro heard the heavy footfalls catching up and held his breath. Then they passed him. He breathed a sigh of relief.

Roseabelle was on the roof. She crept carefully across. When she was at the edge, she dipped down. The guards were about three feet away from the door. Roseabelle leaned over the side and motioned for Jessicana to come up.

She heard a flap of feathers and then a squeal and a flurry of steps. A few minutes later, Jessicana was at her side.

"Don't tell me you flew." Roseabelle said. Jessicana sheepishly nodded. "Come on," Roseabelle hissed.

She pointed at the guards, then pantomimed herself climbing down the wall behind the guards and opening the door, then running. Roseabelle motioned that the guards would notice and run after her.

Jessicana looked at her like she was crazy. "Then what?" she mouthed.

Roseabelle motioned that Jessicana could sneak in and hide. The cloaksmen would be busy chasing Roseabelle. She motioned for Jessicana to stay put inside the building. Roseabelle would then get out and then come back in. Jessicana was staring at her like she had lost her mind. Roseabelle sighed and mouthed, "Get ready."

She went to the edge and carefully turned around. She put her foot on a jagged spot, then found a round stone to place her hand.

She continued to her put her hands and feet in good positions. When she got down, she couldn't believe her plan was working. Her back was to the Darvonians. They hadn't even noticed she was there. Carefully she lifted the latch on the door and opened it.

It creaked.

Roseabelle hurled it open and charged down a narrow passageway, which led to a hall with seven doors.

Roseabelle threw open one door and ran through, not even caring to shut it. It led to another hall with six doors.

She opened one of the doors and ran through, this time shutting it. It led to a room with five doors. She opened the nearest one and sprinted in. That led to a room with four doors. She pushed open one. It led to a hall with three doors. She tore through it. Inside was a room with two doors. She opened one. It led to a room with one door. Roseabelle reached for the knob and . . . it was locked.

Roseabelle gulped and then raced to a shadow in the corner of the room. She pictured the cave and then stomped her foot. She felt as light as air and whisked past drifts of cold and warm air.

Then she landed in the stony cave that she and her friends were staying in. Roseabelle sat down and desperately hoped Jessicana went along with the plan.

* * * * *

Jessicana was confused. What in the world was Roseabelle aiming to do? It did not make sense. Then Jessicana remembered that Roseabelle was Meta-Mord. She was likely to use one of her special powers. The very thought made Jessicana feel better as Roseabelle climbed down the wall.

She was terribly brave to do that. *Roseabelle was taking every risk to save Danette*, Jessicana thought in admiration.

If Roseabelle wanted her to do something, then she would do it. When Roseabelle opened the door, Jessicana watched with bated breath.

She watched as her friend flung open the door and raced inside. The Darvonian guards whirled around and shouted something that sounded like Daronese, the secret Darvonian language. Jessicana had been learning the basics and she translated it

"There's a bee in my skirt!"

Jessicana was sure that that was not what he meant. As they chased after Roseabelle, shouts came from the building. "There's a bee in my skirt. There's a bee in my skirt!"

When the shouts diminished, Jessicana placed a hand on a rock and begun her climb down. When she was on the ground, she cautiously went inside. She reached a hall with multiple doors.

Jessicana chose one on the far right and went through. It was empty except for a tall wooden cabinet and a small worktable. Jessicana opened the cabinet and prepared to step in when she realized that the cabinet had no floor.

She peered inside and saw that it was a long way down. Jessicana turned into a parrot and descended.

Jessicana continued to fly down, all the while wondering if the tunnel ever stopped. Shortly after her feet brushed against stone, Jessicana turned back into a girl.

She looked up. Even at her present state, the usual floor line was several feet above her. Jessicana looked down. It was too dark to see anything. She brushed her hand against what seemed like a floor. It was smooth with the exception of a little notch sticking up. She pulled on the notch. Jessicana gasped. *I have to tell Roseabelle. But how?* she thought.

It was a hidden trapdoor. Jessicana's mind was racing. What could it lead to? Another village? Where Kinetle lived? Perhaps a secret meeting place? Could it have something to do with Danette? Where was Roseabelle?

She wished she would get here right away. This was a truly important discovery.

* * * * *

Roseabelle was sitting on the cave floor, pondering her next action. She wanted to help Jessicana, but what if she ended up with the Darvonians? She had to wait though she did not like it at all. Deciding to do something useful, she pulled the trutan out of her pack and started to draw.

Soon Roseabelle was standing in front of three black robes. She put one on. She found one with just the right fit. She saved the other two for her friends, putting them in Jessicana's backpack.

She sat down and ventured to a shadow and thought hard of the hallway with seven doors. She stomped her foot.

Roseabelle landed in the hall. She passed the door that she had entered earlier and opened a different one. Empty.

Roseabelle tried another door. Dust and dirt but nothing else.

She opened another. It was filled with empty crates and boxes.

A different door had cans of a thick, creamy paste behind it. Roseabelle pocketed a small jar.

A different room held a few binders filled with folders. She tucked one in her robe. The last door she entered had a table and a tall cabinet. The cabinet door was ajar. Roseabelle walked over to it and peered inside. There was no floor.

She scuttled inside, keeping her hands on the wall. She was slipping but kept her grip tight. One arm slipped off the wall. Roseabelle clawed frantically at the stone.

She fell, screaming all the way down. Then shaky, skinny arms broke her fall. Kind aqua-blue eyes stared into hers. "Jessicana?" she asked weakly.

Then everything went black.

Roseabelle sat up. Where was she? What had happened? Then she remembered. Jessicana had saved her! Through the darkness Roseabelle saw Jessicana bending over her, pouring water on her forehead.

"Roseabelle," Jessicana cried, "you're awake. I need to show you something." Jessicana pointed to the panel. "Look," she said. "It's a secret entrance."

Roseabelle's heart leaped. What if it led to her mother?

* * * * *

Astro was in the rock cavity, trying to navigate where he was. He had seen a patch of rocky land close to both the cave and the village. Maybe that was where he was.

He hoped his desperate action had been enough for his friends to get to the building. The question was where would he go next? The cave would be too risky. The village was out of the question. But he couldn't just stay put! He had to think of something. He sighed, wishing he could escape without a trace.

A few hours later, Astro was bored. It was dark, and he was hungry, thirsty, tired, and uncomfortable, and his throat was parched and sore.

He knew he should leave soon. The cloaksmen must have given up by now. They were most likely guarding the city. How would he get in? All these questions.

Just then, a few pairs of large, pounding footsteps went by him, and Astro curled up against the wall. He realized that two Darvonians were talking to each other, grins on their faces. "I'm the one who followed her daughter!"

"And what's the significance of that? I actually captured her!"

"Don't forget, I'm the one who put up the defenses in the castle. I had to construct the maze in front of the dungeon."

Astro's ears perked up. Could these two Darvonians be talking about Danette? He went through what they had mentioned; a castle, a dungeon, and a maze. His heart lifted. Could that be where Danette was being kept?

Mustering up his courage, he stepped out of the opening. The coast was clear. He set off for the village.

* * * * *

"I think we should go in," Roseabelle said eagerly.

"Wait a minute. We need to wait for Astro. He'll help us."

Roseabelle threw up her hands. "Astro. I forgot about him. Don't worry. I'll be back."

She ran to a shadow in the corner and pictured the village wall. She stomped her foot, and flashes of sky and land passed by her.

When she opened her eyes a boy was coming to the wall. He stopped. Roseabelle tried to get a better look. The boy had spiky black hair and green eyes. Astro ran to Roseabelle.

"Come on," she whispered. "Jessicana and I found something. Oh, yeah one minute. Wait here."

Roseabelle retreated into the shadows and pictured the cave and shadow tumbled. A few moments later she was standing next to Jessicana's backpack. She hefted all the blankets in her own pack and then pictured the wall and shadow tumbled. As she came out of the shadow next to the wall, and seeing Astro, she said, "Let's go."

The cloaksmen were still out looking for him so they weren't back yet. They both scampered up the wall and then dropped down. They ran to the building. Voices were muttering inside.

Taking a deep breath, Roseabelle and Astro draped the robes over their shoulders and opened the door.

Heavy footsteps were coming their way. Roseabelle pulled Astro through the passage and to the hall. One of the doors was starting to open. Roseabelle opened a door and threw herself inside. Astro followed her. They had just closed it when they heard footsteps clomping out.

They waited until the footsteps were gone. "Here," Roseabelle whispered. She turned around and pointed to the cabinet.

"Roseabelle, Astro, is that you?" a voice called from below.

"Yes," Astro announced.

"Come on down," came the reply. "Roseabelle, there is rope in my pack," said Jessicana.

Roseabelle pulled it out and tossed one end down. It tightened as Jessicana grasped it. It slacked a bit as Jessicana tied a loop in her end and fastened it around a large stone protruding from the inside.

Up above, Astro tied the rope to his waist. "Here I go," he said nervously. He pushed off from the cabinet and disappeared from view.

"Are you down?" Roseabelle called.

"Yep. That was cool, but remind me to never do that again. That must have been what, a sixty-foot drop? It was still a thriller though."

"Whatever," Roseabelle muttered.

The rope came back to her, and she caught it. She looped it around her waist and pushed off. She was plummeting straight down. Roseabelle seriously thought she was going to hit the floor. When she landed, she instantly tore the rope off her.

"You don't need to remind me to never do that again," she said shrilly. Jessicana stood up.

"I showed Astro the trapdoor," she said.

Roseabelle nodded. "Good."

"I think we should go," Astro said excitedly.

"Quick, let's find out where this leads."

He was already lowering himself down. Roseabelle followed him, then Jessicana.

CHAPTER 10

Moformi

I**T WAS A DARK PASSAGEWAY. T**HE FRIENDS HAD TO crawl low or hit their heads on the ceiling. It became wider with every step and soon it was a clearing.

They sat down to have lunch. Or dinner. Or breakfast. Roseabelle had no idea what time of day it was or how much time had passed.

As Astro and Jessicana ate their honey nuts, Roseabelle decided to creep ahead. The clearing led back to a passageway.

The passageway then split into two.

"Astro! Jessicana! Come here!" Roseabelle called. There was some rough scuttling, and then her friends appeared.

"What?" they asked.

"Which way should we go through?" Roseabelle asked.

"That way," they said, pointing opposite directions.

Roseabelle sighed. The left-hand passage had a set of steps going down. Roseabelle shook her head. How many feet below were they?

The other passage went a few feet out and then came to a halt at an iron door.

"Split up," she ordered. "Jessicana and I will go down the steps. Astro, you can go to the door."

They trotted obediently to where they had been assigned. Roseabelle went to the stairs with Jessicana.

She stepped on one.

It became jellylike and squirmed around. Roseabelle quickly withdrew her foot. The red substance squirmed to the other step, which turned jellylike too. The substance combined and squirmed to another step. That turned into red jelly too. Roseabelle backed away.

Whatever it was, she was certain that it wasn't Benotripia's strawberry jam.

The jelly was on the tenth step now and almost to the bottom.

Squirm, swish. Squirm, swish.

Five steps left.

Swish, swish.

Three steps left.

Squirm, squirm.

Two steps.

Swish, squirm.

One step.

Soon all the steps were red jelly. The jelly started to bubble and hiss. It grew and grew.

"Run!" shouted Jessicana.

They tore out of the passage and to Astro. He was pounding the door. He turned to them. "Locked," he said simply.

"Locked!" Roseabelle screamed. "Look what's behind us!"

Astro swiveled around. His face paled. "Guys, let's get out of here!" Roseabelle and Jessicana turned around to see what he was looking at. It was a monster that looked like it was made of the jelly substance they had seen. It had a wide forehead, squinty eyes, a large nose, and a huge, gaping mouth.

It started toward them, its mouth wide open. "Jessicana!" Roseabelle shouted. "Give me your backpack!"

Jessicana threw it at Roseabelle, too stunned to speak. Roseabelle ripped open the pack and pulled out silk gloves and the dragocone ray. She pulled on the gloves and took the ray.

"Astro," she said, "blast open the door. Get to safety. Read in Jessicana's books. See if there's anything that tells us how to fight a jelly monster. Go!"

Roseabelle swung the ray at the monster. It hit its enormous belly and the jelly broke apart for just a minute. Roseabelle took the opportunity to slash at the monster. Its mouth and eyes fell away from its body. They quickly squirmed back together, this time forming a slug with a huge mouth. The slug snapped at Roseabelle, but she dodged it and struck again with the ray.

It caused the shell of the snail to detach, but the monster rejoined itself, this time into a dragon. The dragon blew jelly fire at her.

Roseabelle sidestepped out of the way, but some of the curling red mass brushed her shoulder. It began to spread, causing searing pain.

"Astro," she cried, "is there anything on it?"

"Hold on, Roseabelle. Hold on." The pain had spread down to her hand and now was inching its way up to her neck. Roseabelle gritted her teeth and swung again.

The dragon hissed another spurt of the flame, but Roseabelle batted it away with her ray. The dragon pounced on Roseabelle, and she leaped out of the way.

"Astro," she called, "I need info on this now!"

"I have some," he replied. "This is a creature called 'Moformi,' or a jelly creature. You might find it as a harmless metal shape but once touched it will turn to its true form. It can morph into any shape. The jelly it is made out of can be poisonous. After a while, it will start to harden and become metallic. If it hardens in a shape of a monster it will be invulnerable. To defeat it will require us to morph it to an everyday shape such as a small toy or a tool. If done, it will only awaken again if a living hand touches it," Astro read.

"Uh-oh," Roseabelle said, glancing down at the red fluid flowing on her body. "I'd better defeat this guy quick." She looked up and saw the dragon's head turn gray and hard. She gulped. "Let's do this thing," she said.

She charged the Moformi raising her dragocone ray and then bringing it back down again. The monster swiped a claw at her but not before separating its body from its head. She slashed at its body again and again. She chopped with all her strength, and soon curvy pieces of jelly were squirming around.

Every time one tried to rejoin, Roseabelle slashed it up into tinier pieces. Soon one piece was pure metal. Then another. And another. Roseabelle worked hard until every last strip of jelly was metal once again.

She sighed with relief. But then she looked down at her body. The jelly was nearly down to her heart. She ran to Astro. She pointed at it. "The slime won't turn back into metal until it is off my body. It's poison."

Astro gulped and jostled Jessicana who had been emotionally petrified by the sight of the Moformi. She blinked then said. "W-what?" she asked shakily.

"You're the medicine girl," Astro said. "Roseabelle has poison coursing through her veins. You have to help."

Roseabelle was feeling woozy. She swayed on her feet. She couldn't hear what Astro was saying. She saw Jessicana reach over and pull something out.

She frantically went over to Roseabelle and shoved something that tasted like sour syrup in her mouth. Roseabelle gagged and spit it out, but Jessicana shoved some more in. Roseabelle let herself swallow it.

Her focus got a little better. Jessicana gave her more of the stuff. Soon Roseabelle was back to normal.

"Jessicana," she coughed. "What was that medicine? Only expert healers can get their hands on that kind of medicine. Wait . . . are you a healer? I thought you could only become a healer once you are old enough to do the training."

"Well, you know when you're twelve and you graduate from Power Training Academy, you go to an ESOK Academy."

"Yes, Jessicana, I know that," Roseabelle said impatiently. "It stands for 'Expert Schools for Older Kids.' But why are you a healer?"

"Because my mom was. I wanted to be her apprentice by helping her with her tasks. I did them so well that she let me try a simple concoction. It worked perfectly. I performed greater tasks until Mom decided to talk to your mom, and she confirmed me a healer. When Danette saw my talents, we had a proper ceremony, and I got my certificate. My dream has always been to be the Head Healer in Benotripia," Jessicana explained.

Roseabelle shook her head. "And I never knew." She nodded at Astro. "How'd you find out?"

Astro shrugged sheepishly. "I walked in on her while she was preparing a mixture for delirium. She had no choice but to explain."

"And when was it that you found out?" Roseabelle asked.

"When we were all eight, thirty days after I received my certificate," Jessicana said. "Anyway that isn't important. You know the truth, so let's move on."

They all looked at the dark way forward. They pulled on their backpacks and trooped on.

The passage got thinner until it stopped. Above was a blank wall. Instinctively Roseabelle pushed on it.

CHAPTER 11
Cart Ride

THERE WAS A RUMBLING NOISE AND THE WALL moved. The way was now clear, up to ground level. Roseabelle gave them a "stay put" sign and climbed up.

The room was made of stone and had a single oil lamp glowing on a small table. She beckoned for them that the coast was clear.

Jessicana and Astro climbed up.

"Come on," Roseabelle mouthed.

She led them to a stone door. Roseabelle pushed on it tentatively.

It opened up to a wagon. The back of it was facing them. In front was a short Darvonian with his back turned to them.

They dove into the back. It smelled of straw, and

Roseabelle saw a group of crates filled with black fruit of all different shapes and sizes.

The straw was enough to cover Roseabelle and her friends. They felt the cart jostle and then move forward. It was a long ride. It seemed to be endless.

When Roseabelle peeped her head out of the cart, the sun was rising. She was hungry, so she took a mango from her pack and ate it.

She thought that they really needed to draw on the trutan. They had illustrated a bit when in the passage, but since then they hadn't taken a pen to the trutan.

The cart came to a stop. Roseabelle shared a look with Jessicana, which showed they were thinking the same thing: *We need to get out of here!* Roseabelle saw Astro embedded in the straw.

He was pawing at it and raising his head to the surface. "No, Astro," Roseabelle hissed, but before she could take action, he had risen to the air.

His head came back under. "Get out," he whispered urgently.

"How?" Jessicana hissed.

"Just go," Astro whispered, "his back is turned. Go."

Roseabelle and Jessicana scrambled at the straw and rose to the surface. Astro had been right; the old Darvonian's back was turned.

They got out of the cart and stepped onto black pavement. They ducked behind the old wheelbarrow.

The old Darvonian man turned around, and Jessicana peered over the side.

She leaned back to Roseabelle and whispered, "He's loading the fruit onto another cart. Astro's still in that one. If the man pulls out enough crates, he could be exposed."

"Let's hope Astro gets back out soon," Roseabelle whispered.

When the old man was loading a fat crate of fruit, Astro leaped out and came tumbling down right on top of Roseabelle.

"Ouch," she grunted. Jessicana pulled Astro down and gave him a *you-don't-always-have-to-be-such-a-show-off* look.

Luckily the man who was loading the fruit hadn't heard Astro. He absentmindedly carried fruit back and forth from his cart to the other.

When he was done, he began to steer his cart around. The friends clung to the back, and when it was facing the opposite cart, they dove in.

Astro pumped in the air and silently slid into the straw. Roseabelle and Jessicana did likewise.

A few hours later, Roseabelle looked above the straw to see where they were going and saw the scenery for the first time. They were in a sea of dry tree trunks tangled and matted together, their branches sharp and pointy. They had no leaves or buds or fruit. They were just bare. Up ahead Roseabelle spotted a valley. They were heading toward it.

She was wondering if they would ever find her mother. She sank back into the straw and fell into a tiresome sleep.

Roseabelle was having a weird dream. She was on a boat on Blackwater Sea traveling to Darvonia. She had no idea why, but the voyage seemed very important.

On the boat was a Darvonian. He was following her every command. It was a little strange, but she didn't mind until he started saying, "Yes, Sheklyth." "Of course, Sheklyth." "May I help you, Sheklyth?" "Is there anything you require, Sheklyth?"

Roseabelle realized she was wearing a black hood. What was going on? She pulled up her long sleeve. Her skin was pale and her fingers were too long.

"Slow down," she barked at the Darvonian. Her voice was different. She leaned over the side of the boat and looked at her reflection in the black water. It was hard to see, but it was there.

When she saw her reflection, Roseabelle was looking at the face of her trainer, Shelby. "What? I'm Roseabelle," she exclaimed in Shelby's voice. "This isn't right!"

The wind howled as if with laughter, the waves splashing in her face. Then she woke up.

Roseabelle started fiddling with some straw.

What had been going on in her dream?

She had been Shelby, for sure. But had the Darvonian known she was Shelby?

What did it mean? If he had known that Shelby was a Benotripian, well, any Darvonian would have hurled a Benotripian overboard immediately.

But the Darvonian had been calling Shelby a different name. What was it again?

Shirley?

No, that wasn't it.

Seklt?

No, that didn't seem right either.

But how could Shelby have concealed her identity? It made no sense. Maybe it had just been a silly dream with no meaning.

But all the same, Roseabelle had a terrible nagging feeling that Shelby wasn't exactly what she seemed.

* * * * *

Astro was looking at the stars. They were still the same as they were in Benotripia.

He thought guiltily of his parents. Astro's mother had been due back home a week from the day they had left for Darvonia. She was surely frantic by now.

And his dad—well, he was too busy with his job to worry about Astro.

Astro was an only child like Roseabelle. He knew that while Jessicana always complained about her two sisters and three brothers, she was truly lucky to have them. They had gone with her parents on vacation since all of them had graduated from ESOK and were much older.

Astro wished that his parents could see him now. He was no longer the gawky ten-year-old who told jokes and funny stories to get him through the day, no longer the person who was always picked last in every activity and skipped classes because he was tired.

He had grown mentally and physically, putting others before himself and learning to work hard and endure hardships. He had been at sea for more than a week!

And he had Roseabelle to thank for it. He couldn't help admiring her bravery and her determination to find her mother. She could have turned back on the sea voyage or the first step she took on Darvonia. But she held fast and fought with all her might, not losing hope of finding her mother.

And there was Jessicana with her mighty brain. Her talent was extraordinary, and Astro had complete faith in her.

He wanted to help the two girls that were with him. He was occasionally teased at school for hanging out with girls, but he didn't care because he knew secretly the other students were envious. Besides, he would rather hang out with them than anybody else. Roseabelle and Jessicana were different than others. Truly they were.

* * * * *

Jessicana pushed her head through the straw. The cart was moving slowly. And up ahead was a castle. Jessicana blinked. It was still there, and they were moving toward it. It had an enormous drawbridge, which was now closed. She could see three towers that loomed above and five turrets all constructed out of latick. They didn't have castles in Benotripia. Almost everyone was treated as equals.

Though Jessicana still wanted to overlook the castle, she could see a quarry up ahead and since it was light, many Darvonians were probably mining in it. She ducked down into the straw, not knowing what she was facing.

The cart came to a quick halt the following morning. Roseabelle was drawing in the trutan. She put it away. She dug into the straw sideways and found Astro, arms behind his head and snoring loudly, and Jessicana, stretching her arms and yawning.

"Jessicana, I'll wake Astro. Go see what's going on," Roseabelle ordered gently.

Jessicana, now fully awake, popped her head out of the straw, and Roseabelle shook Astro. He woke, and they waited for Jessicana to give them a report. When she dipped down again, she told them, "We're at a castle. I saw it yesterday and I forgot to tell you. There's people everywhere—it's pandemonium."

Astro raised his head a little and then said, "They're selling and trading all sorts of stuff." He looked hopefully at Roseabelle. "Can we go?"

"No," she said.

"Come on," Astro complained, "we have those Darvonian robes and some Benotripian money. We can get Darvonian money from the trutan or maybe trade something we have for things we need. We might even be able to get in the castle. Please?" he added.

"Astro, the whole point of this mission is to rescue my mother. I'm not going to risk some market trip for her freedom. Got it?" Roseabelle said fiercely.

"Didn't you hear what I just said? This might be our free ticket to the castle. I'm almost positive that Danette is here!" Astro argued.

Roseabelle sighed. "Fine, but honestly we have to find out what Darvonian money is before we draw. Astro, you go!"

Astro pulled on his black robe and carefully leapt from the cart.

"I hope this works," Roseabelle muttered to Jessicana. A few minutes later Astro was back, rolling his eyes. "What is it?" Roseabelle demanded.

"Sorry," Astro said with a note of sarcasm, "but I just can't believe it. They have twenty-five kinds of money! I can only remember one. It's half latick and half gold. Talk about exquisite! They can't even build properly, yet they have all this fancy currency."

Roseabelle took the trutan, a bottle of boorsh-berry juice from Benotripia, and a small twig. She took the twig and began to draw a large sack, including heaps of half latick and half gold coins within the sack, onto the trutan.

The three friends then gathered to wait, not noticing the cloaked figures chuckling to themselves outside of the cart.

CHAPTER 12
Dust Draining

WHEN THE COINS WERE COMPLETE, Jessicana and Roseabelle pulled on their cloaks, and Roseabelle tied the sack of money to her waist. They scrambled out of the cart. No one was facing them. They carefully stepped onto the stone pavement.

Roseabelle gaped at the sight. How could anything be so horrifying and amazing at the same time?

There were stalls and booths in every direction, and cloaked figures were selling their goods behind them. One booth was selling weapons, including swords, daggers, spears, bows and arrows, trapitas, thepgiles, and drago-cone rays. Another was trading stories written on trutan.

Astro picked a trutan up and, after reading a few lines, turned green and put it down. He shuddered.

"Who would ever want to read that?" he muttered filled with distaste.

One booth was selling *A Journey*, apparently Kinetle's autobiography, while another sold dried skins and furs. Darvonians were selling food, water, political guides, and even some things that Roseabelle thought she would get sick over.

"Let's get what we need and go," she whispered to Jessicana. "I'm getting restless to go the castle."

Jessicana nodded and told Astro.

Roseabelle went to a weapon stall and asked the Darvonian how many she could get if she paid him a coin. He replied gruffly that it was a cutthroatine coin and with it she could buy nine swords, three spears, five quivers of arrows, two crossbows, one trapita, and a dragocone ray.

Roseabelle was flustered and said she would only take a dagger, a crossbow and quiver of arrows, and a spear. He gave her two handfuls of pure silver coins in change and told her to move it. She slipped the coins in her sack and bought a sheath for her dagger.

After purchasing a leather belt, a canteen of luke-warm water, and a red robe, she met her friends at some other stalls.

Jessicana had gotten *A Journey* and a political guide.

Astro had purchased a few Benotripian birds that had clearly been stolen (and he planned to set them free) and a small dragocone ray.

A few minutes later, they stood in front of the draw-bridge of the castle.

"So Mister let's-go-into-the-castle-and-everything-will-work-out-fine, what's the plan?" Roseabelle asked, her voice low.

Astro gulped. He cleared his throat and said loudly, "We would like to speak with Kinetle immediately."

The bystanders didn't hear, but a magnified voice rumbled, "What is the cause?"

This had better work, Roseabelle thought.

"Uh, for EFID," Astro confirmed.

Roseabelle and Jessicana gaped at him. How did he know what to say?

"Come in," the voice said.

The drawbridge lowered. Once in the courtyard, Roseabelle whispered, "How did you know that?"

"Hush, there's no time to explain," Astro said quietly.

They crossed the courtyard and went up to the castle looming above. The friends looked back at the draw-bridge. It was up again. They shuddered as the large castle door in front opened by itself. They stepped inside and viewed their surroundings.

The windowless room they were in was built of dark, sturdy stone. They didn't have time to notice much more because Roseabelle's face turned bright green, Jessicana's legs slipped under her, and Astro had to lean onto the wall for support. A horrible stench was filling the room and drenching the three friends in disgusting odor. Roseabelle gasped for clean air. The smell was a thick mixture of spoiled meat, rotten eggs, garbage, and wet wool.

Jessicana and Astro gasped continually. "Can't . . . breathe," Jessicana coughed. She was on her knees, clutching her throat. Her eyes rolled back into her head and she collapsed against the stone floor.

Astro was starting to cough too. "Roseabelle . . . you're Meta-Mord . . . do something," he whispered weakly. He too slumped onto the floor.

Racking coughs filled the air as Roseabelle thought about her powers. What could she do? The smell was making them lose consciousness. Suddenly it came to her. She knew she could drain and dissolve things into thin air.

She had only done it once because it took tons of energy from her, but now it was her only option. Just as dizziness nearly overcome her, Roseabelle opened her mouth wide and sucked in the air.

The smell began to diminish and the particles vanished completely. Roseabelle scrambled to Astro's side and shook him. Astro sat up.

"That was the most terrible event that's happened in my life," he muttered. He turned to Roseabelle. "What did you do?" he whispered. Roseabelle explained. "That is an incredible power," Astro remarked quietly. "What's it called?"

"Dust draining," Roseabelle answered. "Come on, let's wake up Jessicana. Whatever you told them, Astro, it worked. Enough to get us into the castle, at least," Roseabelle said.

When Jessicana was up, Roseabelle led them forward into the deep bowels of the castle. She realized that they had just entered a minor sitting room. When she opened a heavy stone door, it led to a fork of passages. One led to higher ground, while the other went down. There were a handful of other doors, but Roseabelle saw all different kinds of smoke coming out from under the doors. She didn't have the strength to dust drain again.

"Maybe we should split up," Astro suggested.

"No," Roseabelle said sharply, remembering the jelly creature. "We stay together. This is most likely Kinetle's palace, remember? I say we go up."

"Why?" Astro asked.

"Well, look at the other doors," Roseabelle explained. "See how they're built into the wall? There are so many of them that none of them could have a complicated maze inside. Besides, I don't think my mother is going to be in the very front of the castle. She'd be too easy to get to. And the passage that goes level, well, if you look ahead, it doesn't go far either. That's why we should go up." Roseabelle looked up. "Well, what do you think?" she asked.

"Well," Astro said, "it's a good observation, and it's the only plan we have. We can always go back if something goes wrong or if we reach a dead end." Jessicana nodded her head. "Well, let's continue then," Astro said encouragingly.

Jessicana smiled, and then together they tiptoed up the gloomy passage.

The passage seemed to lead on for what seemed like hours, and then they came to a halt in front of a door with gruesome images carved on it.

Before Roseabelle peered through a crack in the door, Astro noted, "Darvonians don't have the best sense of decoration, do they?"

He chuckled weakly, but no one laughed back. Roseabelle saw a stone floor through the crack, and standing on it were four table legs in the shape of poisonous snakes. Nearby was the grand base of an ornate pot.

Hearing no sounds, Roseabelle cautiously pushed the door open. As she had supposed, a large desk stood in the middle of the stone floor of the room. Beside it was a black pot containing a withered plant. There was a soft chair made of a velvety substance (something Roseabelle guessed was moon panther fur) and a jar of black ink with a pen.

Roseabelle saw that there was a piece of trutan of the desk. On it was written,

S,

What is taking you so long? You have deliberately failed me. Unbelievable! You, my eldest child, of all people! I tell you, that girl is suspecting you. You're not even careful. The little Benotripian was bound to know she was being tricked! You have disgraced me! I want you to come to the castle right away. That girl and her friends need a little talking to. See you soon!

—K

Roseabelle reread the letter with interest. What did *K* mean by "that girl"? Could it be talking about herself? But that was impossible! *K* was obviously a Darvonian and the Darvonians didn't know that Roseabelle and her friends were here. Well, at least that was what she thought.

Then she recalled the name of the leader of the Darvonians. *Kinetle.* Could Kinetle have written this and then forgotten to send it?

Roseabelle gulped and made sure the trutan was positioned in the place where she had found it. She bent down and studied the ink. By the look of it, the ink was wet, which meant Kinetle had written the letter quite recently.

Roseabelle shivered. What if Kinetle was in the palace? "Come on," she said to Jessicana and Astro. "Let's move it. I have a creepy feeling about this."

There was another door at the front of the room, and Astro opened it.

Before them stood a maze of passageways, tunnels, and dead ends.

CHAPTER 13

Maze of Danger

W OW," WAS ALL ASTRO COULD UTTER.
"We're supposed to go through there?"
Jessicana asked, her voice strained.

"How?" Roseabelle groaned.

She was about to take a step forward when Astro shouted, "Stop!"

"Astro," Roseabelle hissed, "the castle isn't deserted. There's probably someone here. Now we'll be discovered."

He put a finger on the maze floor. It shuddered, and then a huge chunk of it fell into a deep, dark abyss. Roseabelle looked at Astro.

"Well, it's good you came along. That was one cruel trap."

Astro shrugged. "Darvonians are full of those kinds of things."

Roseabelle tried to think of a solution. She reached inside her robe and pulled out the folder she had taken from the building where the passage had been found. Nothing that could help them there. She plunged her hands in her robes, twisting and grabbing for something. Her hands then closed around a small vial full of black creamy paste.

"I got this from that building," she exclaimed.

She turned to Jessicana. "Do you know what this is?" she asked. Jessicana eyed it quizzically and then pulled a heavy book out of her pack. She flipped pages through the book and then motioned for them to listen.

"Here," she announced, "listen up." Then Jessicana began to read. "*This substance, scientifically called Aphrotykkiedle, or otherwise as known as Lypith, is very dangerous. It is a black, thick liquid/paste that can be used to heal or wound. For healing, spread it over the wound and wait. To cause damage, toss it in cold water and it will solidify. Touch it with a small bar of gold and throw it. It will soon explode. If you pour it on latick, it becomes as heavy as a full-grown man. The full powers of Lypith are yet to be uncovered.*" Jessicana looked up. "Does that help?" she asked.

"Yes," Astro said. He turned to Roseabelle. "Jessicana can fly over the gap. She can fly but not land. Jessicana, you can have a squirt of this Lypith. Let it fall on the latick floor. If it breaks the floor, it means the floor won't support our weight, so fly back over here to help us. If it doesn't, land and help us get across the abyss," Astro ordered, taking charge.

"How?" Jessicana asked.

"Well, you could perhaps drag us along."

"Yeah, and drop you along the way," Jessicana said.

"Oh, so you got a better plan?" Astro asked. Jessicana was silent. "That's what I thought," Astro said.

He poured a little Lypith onto Jessicana's hand, and Jessicana transformed. She flew to the other side and let the black liquid drip from her wing onto the stone. It didn't break and Roseabelle breathed a sigh of relief.

Jessicana flew to Astro and turned back into a girl. She grabbed his shirt and turned into a parrot. Her claws were grasping his shirt. Roseabelle watched with her fingers parted over her eyes. Jessicana flew out onto the trench of blackness.

Roseabelle saw that Astro was weighing her down. She watched in horror as her friends started to slip down. This wasn't going to work. She turned to her backpack and rummaged through it, trying to find something that could help them.

Her hands closed around thick rope. Roseabelle slapped her hand against her forehead. Rope! How could they have forgotten?

She tied it around her waist and flung one end of it to Astro. He caught it and looped it around his wrist. Roseabelle reeled him in like a fisherman reeling in a fish.

When he was safely in the room, she said, holding up the rope, "Forget this?

Astro's face turned red.

"Sorry," he mumbled.

Roseabelle sighed and removed the rope from Astro's wrist. She flung it to the maze and it caught on a patch of stone. Roseabelle dropped and was going down into the trench. Then she stopped in midair. The rope was working. She climbed up it and reached the other side of the maze. She held it out to her friends several feet away.

Jessicana got the message and flew to her. She clutched the rope in her beak and brought it to Astro. Roseabelle watched as Astro tied it around his waist and swung to her. Jessicana flew over. Roseabelle was holding the jar of Lypith.

"Good thinking, Roseabelle!" Jessicana cheered.

"Totally," Astro approved. They turned to the maze. There was a large tunnel leading forward. Roseabelle took the jar and opened it. She took a splotch of Lypith on her fingertip and hurled it forward. The stone didn't break.

They advanced forward. Once through the tunnel, Astro pointed out a fork in the maze. Eleven passages led forward. Roseabelle took a bit more of the Lypith and flung it at a passage on the far right. The stone staggered and then crumbled.

Roseabelle tried the passage next to that. It broke too. Each tried passage crumbled into dust. The last passage was yet to be tried. Roseabelle let the Lypith touch the stone. It stayed. They raced forward.

There were many other drop-offs, and stone breaking echoed throughout the maze. Twice they reached dead ends and had to retrace their steps.

Finally they came to the end: a heavy oak door. When Astro touched the door, it felt ice cold. It surprised him, and he withdrew his hand.

When Jessicana leapt forward, the door was scorching hot.

When Roseabelle touched it, the wood was warning her. It seemed perfectly normal except for the ugly gargoyles on the door, which were staring at her with piercing red eyes. There was a sense of forbiddance in the air. She pushed it open quietly.

Below her was a set of stairs. With each step she took, a faint echo reached her ears.

At the bottom of the steps was a door with metal bars and standing in front of it was—

"Hide!" Roseabelle hissed.

CHAPTER 14
Danette

SHE DRAGGED ASTRO TO THE SIDE, AND JESSICANA hid behind them. Three Darvonians wielding trapitas and thepgiles were guarding the door.

Now that Roseabelle listened, she could hear a sorrowful humming from inside. Roseabelle's heart took a leap. She knew that tone. Tears began to gather in her eyes. It was Danette. After all that searching, she had finally found her. More than ever she wanted to embrace Danette and hear her mother's gentle soothing words that they were going to be okay.

She touched the stone arrows that she had bought and stroked the hilt of her dagger. She handed her spear to Jessicana.

"You'll need it," she whispered. Jessicana nodded gratefully. Roseabelle readied her crossbow with an arrow and watched as Astro pulled on silk gloves and drew his ray. Jessicana set a determined face and swung her spear for practice.

Roseabelle looked at her friends. "On the count of three," she mouthed. She held up one finger, then two, then three, and they burst into action.

Astro tackled a beefy cloaksman on the right. The cloaksman swung his trapita at Astro, but the lightning boy threw down his ray and shot an enormous lightning bolt out of his fingers. The guard was distracted because he had clearly thought that Astro would use his ray. The bolt hit his armor but left a hole in the metal.

The Darvonian slumped to the floor. Astro turned to help the girls.

When Jessicana jumped out, she hoped that she could help. She wasn't much of a fighter. Luckily she was taking down a tall, wiry guard who seemed like a bit of a non-warrior like herself. *Pretty fair*, she thought.

She thrust her spear at him, but it just clanged harmlessly against his armor. With a quick flick of his wrist, the guard sent his thepgile hurling at Jessicana. The bird girl hesitated, then dropped her weapon and turned into a parrot.

The thepgile lodged itself in a block of heavy, gray stone. Jessicana flew up, pecking him. It did nothing really, but it was just enough to buy herself some time as Astro picked up and swung his dragocone ray at him. The cloaked guard was knocked back and he hit the wall behind him. He was soon unconscious.

"Nice work!" cried Jessicana to Astro.

Roseabelle sent an arrow at her opponent. It bounced from his armor and flew back at her. She could have sworn that the guard was wearing two layers of metal armor. He was bulky and covered in sweat. Roseabelle watched as the arrow fell to the floor.

She pretended like she was going to shoot another arrow. Roseabelle dropped her crossbow and stared at a rock on the floor. It rose behind the guard's head.

He began to run to her, winding up his trapita. Roseabelle stared even harder at the stone and it slammed into his helmet. The guard felt it and swatted it. She stared at his helmet. It began to lift higher and then it was levitating above his head.

She fixed her eyes on the stone and it hit the guard's head. He froze and fell down.

Astro and Jessicana rushed over to her. "We got all of them!" Astro cried. "I can't believe it!"

"Let's go get your mom, Roseabelle," Jessicana said.

They rushed to the door. Astro shot a bolt at it, but it bounced back at him. He ducked, and it burned the back wall.

"We need the keys," Roseabelle said urgently. They searched the cloaksmen and found the keys on the belt of the cloaksman Roseabelle had attacked. Roseabelle pushed the door open. Inside was Danette sitting on a hard bed, tapping her foot against the stone.

"Roseabelle!" she cried, her eyes sad and alert. "Go! Get out of here. Get out of the cell. You have to. Listen do it. I'll find a way to get out. Just go."

"I d-don't understand," Roseabelle stammered. There was a squeal behind her. Danette's face was pale. "Go, Roseabelle," she said.

Roseabelle took a step backward, confused. What did her mother mean? They had knocked out the Darvonians back there. There was no danger. The faint sound of a click of a lock sounded.

"Well, well. Come to take a little visit at last?" a cold voice asked. Roseabelle turned around slowly.

CHAPTER 15

Sheklyth

WHEN SHE SAW THE SPEAKER, ROSEABELLE could have fainted. How could this be? It was traumatizing, but Roseabelle knew somehow that it was her. This was the horrible truth.

It was Shelby.

"A little surprised to see me, Roseabelle? Yes, of course. I've been waiting for you. Oh yes, waiting for so long to have this little talk."

"B-but you're a Benotripian," Roseabelle stammered, not believing her eyes. Shelby smirked.

"Being an IB is so useful at times. Benotripians can never tell the difference."

"You're an IB," Roseabelle cried. "But I don't get it. You taught me at the academy. How did you get in if you're a Darvonian?"

Shelby laughed. "Easy. I made sure no one could suspect me by giving them no reason to. I didn't bring any weapons. Or Darvonian marks. IB's look perfectly like Benotripians. Too simple."

Roseabelle was still trying to figure out everything. She realized that Astro and Jessicana weren't in the room with her. They were outside the door, fighting a whole army of Darvonians. She had to get out of here with her mother and her friends. Maybe if she kept talking, she could figure a way out to fight the so-called "Benotripian."

"Why did you come to Benotripia?" Roseabelle asked.

"We had planned to capture your mother long before. I was supposed to keep an eye on you, so you would stay out of the way until it was time. See, if we captured your mother, we knew you would come after her. We could get you and your friends. Benotripians would be frantic for their leader and her daughter. They had already lost Magford. We could make a trade: Benotripia for you. Then at last Benotripia would belong to Darvonia. Carefully devised plan, yes?"

Roseabelle tried to conceal her anger. *Keep talking*, she thought as one hand went to her dagger.

"The feather that Jessicana picked up. What was up with that?" Roseabelle asked, stalling.

"I believe your parrot friend was right about the dream world. You see, you could say Asteran is in some sort of league in us. He was simply communicating with us. When you felt around it, you entered too. You also met my impossible, mad twin, Ugagush," Shelby explained.

Roseabelle remembered Ugagush saying that he was Kinetle's son. Her mouth opened in horror. "Don't tell me you're Kinetle's daughter," she squeaked.

Shelby smiled slyly. "Not only that, but I'm also Darvonia's second-in-command. If something happens to Kinetle, I'm leader."

Roseabelle was in pure shock. How could she have trusted and learned from the heir of Darvonia? How could someone be so cruel? She remembered the letter. S stood for Shelby. The book in the tower room. It had said, "*There is a rumor that one of these children is an IB.*" Roseabelle's stomach lurched.

"The pouch," she said. "Why is it so important?"

Shelby sighed. "Honestly, Roseabelle, you're smarter than that. Think, why is the trutan so important to us?"

Roseabelle's heart sank. Shelby knew what was inside. "So you could build large sea vessels," she suggested.

Shelby shrugged. "Something like that."

"When you were teaching, you wouldn't allow me to feel the emotions of that nasty creature. Why was that?"

"Because," Shelby said, "it was from Darvonia. If you felt its emotions, it would've felt a strong affection toward me. You would probably figure that it was Darvonian, connect two and two, and you know the rest."

"Were you one of the Darvonians that came to get the pouch?" Roseabelle asked, secretly pulling her dagger from inside her robes.

"Nope, that was my sister, Heltonine. She is only seventeen. She's not as brave as perceived. She doesn't always achieve expectations. Heltonine has always looked up to her elder sister, Sheklyth."

"Who's that?" Roseabelle wondered aloud.

Shelby shook her head. "You disappoint me, Roseabelle. My real name is not Shelby. Haven't you realized? I am Sheklyth, daughter of Leader Kinetle, second-in-command of Darvonia.

Roseabelle, still trying to piece it all together, was silent.

Sheklyth looked closely at Roseabelle. "Any more questions before I leave you and your friends in this grimy cell with your mother?"

"Yeah, I have one," Roseabelle said coolly. "How come you were so clueless to let us keep our weapons?" She drew her dagger.

Sheklyth's eyes widened. Roseabelle advanced forward.

"Roseabelle, listen. I don't really see what you can accomplish with that. You can't really harm me," Sheklyth said calmly. She brushed aside her sweeping black robes to reveal a sensible fitting suit of armor to prove her point.

Roseabelle stopped and said, "Darvonians are hopeless. Not only are they mean and spiteful, but they have only cruelty and weapons. Nothing else."

Sheklyth's eyes narrowed. "Who said we only have weapons?" she asked.

"You lack the powers that you trained me on. What else do you have?" Roseabelle asked.

Sheklyth looked pleased. "Something you don't have," she said slyly. She took a deep breath, and then Roseabelle felt an overpowering emotion.

It was fear. Fear like Roseabelle had never imagined before, fear that told her she would never get out of this place. It was penetrating. A blue fog shone from Sheklyth's body, and then it stopped. Roseabelle felt normal.

"That's what we have," Sheklyth said proudly. Roseabelle was stunned. There was a moment of silence. Roseabelle took an arrow and loaded it onto her crossbow.

She lifted it and shot. Sheklyth averted the shot. She smiled in a pleased way and made the penetrating emotion happen again. Roseabelle dropped her weapon.

Fear flooded through her body. She looked at the bars on the door. Astro was still struggling with the Darvonians.

Roseabelle caught his eye. She pantomimed him

sending a bolt flying through the room. Astro cocked his head, showing that he wanted her to repeat the message. Roseabelle showed him again. This time he nodded, showing that he understood.

If the bolt that Astro shot earlier bounced against the door, it will bounce against the walls, she thought. Sheklyth was howling with laughter. Astro stretched forth his finger, and then a streak of sliver and blue came hurling out.

The mass of crackling silver light bounced against the back wall. Roseabelle dived at Sheklyth and wrestled the keys from her. The Darvonian spit in rage and tried to seize the keys. She quickly stopped her pursuit as Astro's stray lightning bolt barely grazed her face and singed off the bottom of her hair. Roseabelle rushed to Danette and pulled her up. She took her mother's hand, and Roseabelle unlocked the door.

"Mom, after being locked up, do you think you can still fly?" she shouted over the sound of fighting. Flying was one of Danette's powers. The other was turning invisible. Danette nodded in response to her daughter's question.

Roseabelle and Danette raced out and locked Sheklyth in. Meanwhile, Astro and Jessicana were dealing with the Darvonians.

Only two were unconscious, but twenty-two fierce Darvonian warriors remained in the fight. Roseabelle's heart sank. The battle seemed to be tipping in the

Darvonian's favor. Roseabelle turned to her mother. "Fly up on the ceiling. You're too weak to fight."

Hugging her mother one last time, she gripped her crossbow and loaded it, sneaking from behind a wall of Darvonians and firing. The arrow made its mark and the Darvonian crashed to the dungeon floor. But Roseabelle's victory was short lived, as his two companions whirled around and sent their thepgiles spinning at her. Roseabelle quickly dodged one, but as the other was aimed at her feet, the blade grazed her shoe, tearing the top part of the leather sandal. Roseabelle wasted no time nocking an arrow on her bow and shooting it at the Darvonians. They deflected it with their thepgiles, and Roseabelle tore off at a run before they could aim again at her.

As Roseabelle secretly crouched between the rows of Darvonians, she realized that Jessicana and Astro were cornered. They were still battling the Darvonians and Roseabelle knew that they were about to tire. Reacting quickly, she fired three arrows at a small group of Darvonians, who collapsed as the deadly missiles penetrated their armor. Astro and Jessicana quickly squeezed through the mass of enemies, Jessicana blocking a warrior's sword strikes while Astro used his ray to burn through a Darvonian's helmet. Roseabelle looked up and saw Danette hovering above them, her tired eyes staring sadly down at them. As the Darvonians closed in on them again, Roseabelle shouted, "Astro, drop your weapon!"

Her vague message came across clear to him; he stretched forth a finger and three large jets of electric light bounced across the room. Half the Darvonians were lying on the ground, the lightning having struck them forcefully. The remaining ones were blocking the exit on the far side of the room.

Roseabelle shouted to her mother. "Fly overhead to the exit!" Danette shook her head, and Roseabelle knew what she was trying to say.

"I won't leave you."

Gathering courage, Roseabelle turned back to the fight and was dismayed to find that Jessicana and Astro, though near the exit, were struggling to escape. All that could be seen was the blur of the figures that were Jessicana and Astro and the glow of Astro's dragocone ray. They were working furiously to keep their enemies far away from them. The dungeon was filled with the sounds of clashing metal.

Jessicana had a cut on her left cheek, and Astro's leg was bleeding; an arrow had nipped his skin while zooming past.

Trying desperately to turn the Darvonians' focus away from her friends, she drew her dagger and, with both perfect agility and speed, hurled it at the Darvonian closest to Astro. It struck the warrior in the leg, and the impact jerked him backward and onto the cold stone floor.

Multiple Darvonians whirled around, and

Roseabelle found herself desperately shooting arrow after arrow at her foes. She was relieved to see that amidst the commotion, Jessicana and Astro had managed to sneak out the doorway. A dozen Darvonians were closing in on her, and Roseabelle knew that she wouldn't be able to hold them off for long. Just as they had formed a tight circle around her, two gentle hands scooped her up into the air, and Roseabelle nearly cried with relief. Danette was encircling the Darvonians, Roseabelle on her back.

Danette shot out of the room and past the Darvonians, eyes firm and focused. The Darvonians, shouting with rage, followed not too far behind the flying mother and daughter. A few feet ahead, Jessicana and Astro were sprinting as fast as they could, covering more ground than they would have in normal circumstances.

"Astro! Jessicana!" Roseabelle shouted. "Follow our lead."

The four Benotripians tore through various passageways, doors, and hallways. Danette and Roseabelle flew; Astro and Jessicana ran. The Darvonians were right at their heels.

Astro suddenly flung open a door and his face filled with hope. "This leads to the courtyard!" he shouted ,and Danette shot through as quick as an eagle. Astro and Jessicana followed behind. Much to their horror, the drawbridge began to rise.

Doubt filled Roseabelle's mind. *"Will we make it?"*

"Astro, get on my back! Jessicana, transform! We're going to have to fly over it!" Danette shouted. Roseabelle wrapped her arms around Danette's neck, and Astro hung on to Roseabelle. Danette lifted into the air.

Roseabelle heard angry shouts of Darvonians and looked back fearfully to the ground. The Darvonians were loading arrows onto bows that had been concealed in their robes. "Mom, they're firing!" Roseabelle screamed.

Danette fought against the harsh wind to fly faster, but just before they soared over the top wooden plank of the drawbridge, the Darvonians pulled back their bowstrings and fired their arrows. A dozen arrows shot toward them at lightning speed. Astro shot a bolt at one but missed. As a bird, Jessicana could dodge the arrows more quickly, but Danette was the most vulnerable target. Ten arrows couldn't withstand the wind and took off in different directions, but two remained strong and battled it. Roseabelle stared in utter horror as the two arrows came zooming at her at top speed.

She had no time to think before the missile headed straight for her arm, where her bow was hanging. The arrow split the bow and Roseabelle sighed in relief but not after seeing the other arrow head right to Danette's shoulder. "Mom!" Roseabelle shouted. A gust of wind blew upward, and the point of the arrow tilted up—cutting through her sleeve. Roseabelle sighed with relief but then grimaced as Danette bit her lip. "Are you all right?" Roseabelle cried out. Danette nodded, and both her daughter and Astro could tell that she was in pain. "It just nipped me," she said, forcing a smile. Roseabelle felt Danette shudder and realized that she was struggling to remain in the air.

Jessicana flew over and tried to support Danette, but it was no use. Although they were gaining momentum in their flight pattern, Danette was starting to fall.

Roseabelle saw the land of Darvonia below whiz past: the market where they had bought supplies and the village that Roseabelle had discovered after arriving in enemy territory. She looked ahead, and her heart skipped a beat. Blackwater Sea was just ahead, and on the shores of the beach were a crowd of two dozen Darvonian warriors, gleaming swords waving in their hands. Danette began to lower herself even more, and Roseabelle whispered to Astro "They haven't spotted us yet. Quick, we need to land without being seen."

He scanned the land below, then pointed to an outcropping of rock. "Under there," he suggested quietly. Danette heard him and aimed for the spot that Astro had indicated. She began to pick up speed and momentum, and soon Roseabelle realized that Danette had enough strength to stop them from crash landing. As the black rock came nearer and nearer, Roseabelle wrapped her arms around her mother's waist. "Hold on," she whispered. Just as the pointed mass of shiny black rock came just a few feet away from Danette's face,

Roseabelle pulled her mother up, and they landed on the dry, dirty beach.

Jessicana landed beside them and Astro hissed "Quick, they're looking our way!"

Danette was so weak that Roseabelle had to gently lift her underneath the covering of the rock. Astro also ducked behind it, and Jessicana flattened herself against the rock wall.

"Roseabelle," Astro whispered, "shadow tumble to the cave and bring back the raft. We'll be waiting for you."

She nodded, immersed herself in the shadow of the rock, pictured the cave, and stomped her foot.

Thankfully, no Darvonians were guarding the cave, and Roseabelle quickly snatched the raft. Taking a quick peek of the exterior of the cave, she crept out and saw that the outcropping of rock that her friends were hiding under was directly below her.

As the Darvonians viewed the area, Roseabelle knew what her only option was. She had to jump to her hiding place.

Roseabelle knew it was risky, but, gathering courage, she aimed for her landing and leapt.

When she landed, she saw a hooded face turn her way and she ducked. Roseabelle glanced around the corner of the rock. The Darvonians knew where they were and were slowly and silently advancing. Terror filled Roseabelle. Escape seemed almost impossible.

She crept around to where her friends were crouching and showed them the raft.

"They know," she whispered. Her friends understood the message. Danette looked more pale than ever.

A crazy idea formed in Roseabelle's mind.

"We're going to have to surprise them," she whispered. "If we jump out suddenly, they'll be distracted for a second. It'll give us a head start." She looked to her friends for approval and they nodded. It was a desperate attempt but their situation was frightening.

Roseabelle gripped the raft and motioned for Jessicana and Astro to take hold of it as well. "I'll help my mother," she whispered to them. Jessicana shook her head.

"No, Roseabelle. It's too risky."

"I'll be fine," she whispered back and put her arms around Danette. "You go first."

Jessicana and Astro darted out of their hiding spot, and Roseabelle heard a shout of rage from the Darvonians. Half carrying, half dragging Danette, Roseabelle emerged and saw that the Darvonians had broken into a full sprint. Roseabelle stared at the beach. It seemed as far away as ever.

Adrenaline rushed through her and she ran, helping Danette across the shore and to her friends and the raft.

The Darvonians were gaining, swords drawn and Roseabelle was losing energy. The sight of her foes gaining on her motivated her to reach Blackwater Sea.

Astro and Jessicana had made it to the water; the oars were in their hands. Their expressions were full of fear and horror. "Roseabelle!" Jessicana screamed as the Darvonians rushed to her.

Using her last bit of energy, Roseabelle tore to the waters and felt the soothing and comforting sensation of water on her ankles. Rushing deeper, she placed Danette on the deck and climbed onto the small watercraft. The Darvonians were now wading in the water. Astro and Jessicana raised their oars and determinedly steered the raft away from the beach and the Darvonians.

Roseabelle and Danette held each other for a long time and didn't let go.

It had been two weeks since they had left Darvonia, and the island of Benotripia was nearing. During the journey, Danette told them all about what had happened.

Roseabelle secretly vowed that she would never let this happen to Danette again. There was a pit of anger in her heart. Roseabelle was still upset about the betrayal of Shelby—or Sheklyth.

She still had the folder from Darvonia and trusted it into Astro's care. He told her that the folder was how he had gotten the information to get inside the castle.

Jessicana even started reading Kinetle's autobiography. After the first few pages, she tossed it bitterly into the ocean.

"I thought it would reveal secret battle plans," Jessicana said wrinkling her nose, "but all it talked about was how much she dislikes Benotripians. It's such a waste of trutan."

When the small group pulled up on shore, the two mottels were there. Jessicana made her transformation and circled them, squawking cheerfully. Astro went to tell everyone what had happened to Danette. Roseabelle and her mother walked around the beach, chatting with their arms around each other.

There were thousands of Benotripians that came to the beach and celebrated. They all made their way to the closest Benotripian village.

CHAPTER 16

Celebration

ROSEABELLE, ASTRO, JESSICANA, AND DANETTE spent a night in Lokomonok, a Benotripian city. Danette was a frequent visitor there, so the residents had no problem housing the three friends.

The following day, Jessicana's family and Astro's parents came to Lokomonok. Astro's father said he was only here to interview his son for *The Tropical Times*, but Astro knew better.

Jessicana's siblings praised her. Jessicana was so stunned because she had never heard a word of goodwill from any of her brothers or sisters. The eldest child, Henryl, couldn't stop patting her back.

That night, Astro and his father (who both had the same power) shot brilliant, silver and blue lightning bolts into the sky like fireworks. They went so high into the sky that probably all of Benotripia saw them, even if they were tiny specks in the distance. Danette then decided to travel to Central Square to make an announcement to the people of Benotripia.

Naturally, not all of them would come, but the news would pass along. Roseabelle, Danette, Jessicana and her family, and Astro and his parents traveled to Central Square. The next day, Danette stood on a high rock facing a large multitude of people.

She told them how she had been drawn into captivity by the Darvonians and how they brought her there. The Benotripians listened intently. Danette stopped in her speech. "But this is not all of the story. May I invite my rescuers up here. Make way for Jessicana Wingling, Astro Jagged-Light, and Roseabelle Leading-ton." Jessicana, Astro, and Roseabelle climbed up the stone steps embedded in the rock and joined Danette.

Danette turned to face them. "Would you please tell us the rest of the story?" she requested.

The three nodded. Danette backed away. Jessicana went first, telling them her version of the story. Astro went next. Roseabelle shared her part last, and the audience gasped and screamed more than ever.

When they finished, Danette stepped up. "Thank you," she said solemnly, "for sharing that with us. But before you sit back down I would like to award you."

A Benotripian dressed in green went up to them and handed Danette a wooden box.

She opened it and pulled out a medal made of gold. Engraved on the surface was a parrot feather with a potion bottle. She gestured to Jessicana. The parrot girl blushed and bowed her head so Danette could place it on her neck. "For quick wit and healing talent," Danette said loudly. The Benotripians clapped.

Danette pulled another medal from the box. It was fashioned from silver and had a large lightning bolt on the front. "For profound bravery," Danette announced, resting the medal on Astro's neck.

There was another roar of applauding. Danette pulled one last medal from the box. This one was the most majestic of all. Roseabelle couldn't quite place what it was made of. It was swirling with many colors. Roseabelle could make out a large island with many twists and turns. Beside it was a scepter. "For outstanding leadership," Danette called. She put the medal on Roseabelle.

The clapping went on for at least five minutes. Roseabelle hugged Danette and Jessicana. She grinned at Astro.

"You know, after this," Roseabelle said to them, "I don't think I'll be able to stand going back to my normal schedule."

Astro sighed. "You're right," he said. "It really was a great adventure."

From behind the stage, a red-haired man watched

the auburn-haired girl who had grown so much since the night he had made a promise to Danette. Only part of that promise had been fulfilled.

Discussion Questions

1. If you were faced with Darvonian opponents, what strategies, powers, and weapons would you use to defeat them?

2. If you were a son or daughter of Danette and you discovered your mom was captured by the Darvonians, what would you do?

3. When Astro fell asleep on watch when the friends were traveling to Darvonia by sea, what were the consequences? What would have happened differently if Astro *had* stayed awake?

4. If you were a Benotripian, what power(s) would you like to have? How would you use your power(s)?

5. What was Jessicana and Astro's friendship like with Roseabelle?

6. If you were faced with the danger of making a choice between two paths, which path would you take? Or would you choose to go back altogether?

About the Author

MCKENZIE WAGNER IS ELEVEN YEARS OLD and has adored reading since she was four. Her love of books inspired her to write a book of her own, and she completed the first book of The Magic Wall Series, *The Magic Meadow and the Golden Locket* at age seven and the second book, *The Blue Lagoon and the Magic Coin*, shortly thereafter. She has now expanded her writing to appeal to kids of all ages. She wishes to obtain an English degree and teach and continue in her pursuit of her love of writing. She currently resides in Utah with her mom, dad, and her eight-year-old brother, Ty.